Six Chapters . of . . . A Man's Life

By

Victoria Cross,

Author of "Anna Lombard,"
"Paula," etc., etc.

The Walter Scott Publishing Co., Ltd.
London and Felling-on-Tyne
New York: 3 East 14th Street

THIRTY-NINTH EDITION.

Preface

THE following pages from a human life came
into my hands after that life had ceased to be,
and from the terrible story of reckless trans-
gression and its punishment contained in them,
it seemed to me that Humanity might learn
some of those lessons which Life is ever striving
to teach it. If this should be so, the error and
the agony of the one who left this short record
of wasted days will not have been wholly useless. And that this record may stand as a
lasting protest against all egoism, all love of
love for the sake of pleasure to the lover,
instead of the all-glorious and selfless love
which desires only the well-being of the loved
one, is my whole aim and hope in presenting
it to the public.

VICTORIA CROSS.

'Ω παιδες ἦ τοι Κύπρις οὐ Κυπρις μόνον
ἀλλ' ἔστι πολλῶν ὀνόματων ἐπώνυμος
ἔστιν μὲν "Αιδης ἔστι δ' ἄφθιτος βία
ἔστι δὲ λυσσα μαινὰς ἔστι δ' ἱμερος
ἄκρατος ἔστ' οἰμωγμος . . .

Six Chapters of
A Man's Life.

CHAPTER I

THE charts were all spread out upon the table;
the midnight gas burned steadily above my head;
my pencil traced a dotted line down the paper
under my hand.

"What is she like?" I asked, continuing the
conversation, but without looking up from the
maps.

"She's called Theodora."

"That does not tell me much. Do you mean
she is like Gibbon's Theodora?"

"Bother Gibbon! you know I never read
him. Well, it's difficult to say what she is
like. She is tall, and with a bend-about sort of
figure, don't you know? I don't know what
you call it. Features straight as a billiard cue,

I

and the most thundering eyes you ever saw; and then her eyebrows, they start from her nose, go up to the middle of her forehead nearly, and then come down to her ear!"

"Dear me, what a remarkable person! And I suppose you are much smitten with her?"

"Yes, I don't mind confessing to you that I am; but it's no use. She does not see anything in me."

Hardly her fault, I thought involuntarily, glancing over my friend's five feet two of stature and head of reddish hair.

"But I should like to have the kudos of introducing you to her, I should really."

"What's the use? You know women bore me," I said, leaning back in my chair and pushing the point of my pencil idly up and down the margin of a map.

"Yes, but I should like you to see this one. She's so queer. I am not asking you to fall in love with her. I want you to see her. She's got a moustache."

I laughed.

"She'd be awfully flattered if she heard you

2

describing her," I said. "I suppose you mean a duvet imperceptible, eh?"

"No, I don't mean anything imperceptible," returned Digby doggedly, kicking the bars of the grate. "It's so perceptible that you can see it all across the room. It would spoil most women I know, but it doesn't seem to spoil her. Well, will you come on Friday?"

"I really don't see any object," I said coldly.

What a bore he was, staying gossiping here about his tiresome women, wasting my time!

"She said there was not a good-looking man in town. I said I knew one. She said, introduce him, and I promised I would. You must come. I am sure she'll like you."

"What a happiness for me!" I said ironically. "Well, all right then, I'll come"—feeling I should never get rid of him,—"I'll be there about ten. Now, good-night, old chap; I must get on with my work."

When he was gone I resettled myself and worked on for a couple of hours.

It was rather peculiar work I was doing—a

mixture of geography, archæology, and theory of surveying, all combined. I had obtained a commission from a company, then only recently started, for exploring and excavating in the neighbourhood of the site of Nineveh, and it wanted only three weeks now to the date fixed for my leaving England. It would not by any means be the first time I found myself in the East. Nearly a fourth of my twenty-eight years had been spent there, and I and the East agreed.

The company for the exploration of subterraneous Mesopotamia, as they called themselves, could not have found a man more suited to their present needs than myself, and in consideration of my "points" they were going to give me generous terms. Four hundred for each winter season for the next three years was to be paid to my private account, and all expenses for hire of workmen, necessary travelling, and so on were borne by the company. My actual appointment in their service began from the next autumn, that is to say in September, and it was now January.

A Man's Life

But I was going at once, partly from a habitual restlessness that always comes over me when I have been long in England, and partly because I loved the work I was going to, and had no idea of grudging a few months' extra prospecting without pay. I was glad I had obtained the post, and I felt myself thoroughly fitted for it. My love for the work and my knowledge of the country and the climate were the three advantages that weighed heaviest, perhaps, with the company. It was known that I was a sort of salamander, for which it was impossible to find an unendurable degree of heat. Even in the full blaze of a Mesopotamian summer I had kept my health, while the Europeans round me had sickened, fled, or died. And a man who does not want sick leave in the middle of his work, and who has no tendency to cry off when the thermometer rises over 100°, is a man to be prized. Next in my favour came my conversance with the languages of the East, and my known power of making myself popular with every class of the natives.

At twenty-two, when I had just taken my

degree at Oxford, my father died, and a loose five thousand came into my hands. With this five thousand I started for the East and travelled there, wandering where the fancy took me, studying the languages, amusing myself with the various forms of pleasure that the different cities offered or permitted, and acquiring a sympathy with the character and fashions of the Eastern. At the end of six years I came back to England with only a hundred a year to call my own, and eager to find some means of supplementing it. Thanks to the influence of my father's friends, one of whom had a share in the company, I had secured this post from the Sub. Mes. Ex. Association, which would see me over the next three years, long enough for me to look ahead. I seldom did more than consider the passing hour, and tried to live its sixty minutes to the utmost. I agreed not with Horace, who bids us live to-day, but with Martial, who warns us that even to-day is late to begin, and wise is the man who has lived yesterday. And these past six years had been an almost unbroken

A Man's Life

stretch of easy, careless, pleasant, irresponsible existence, which had helped to make me what I was now—selfish, easy-going, loose in morals, and averse to every sort of restriction, responsibility, or tie, and ambitionless.

In the East, where Death looks out with the eyes of fever from every summer sky, with the eyes of cholera from every stream; where a death-blow may be in any shaft of sunlight, and the poison of death in any of the faint, sickly odours in the nostrils; where diseases are so rapid, and the summons to the grave so sudden; where you dine with your dearest friend, strong in health, at night, and before breakfast in the morning you may meet his *cortège* passing to the burial-ground; there, where these things are, ambition wanes, and one falls into the habit of setting little store by to-morrow. In England life seems more secure, or at any rate one knows that generally there is a more civil and elaborate notice to quit, and time allowed to set one's house in order. But in the East Death walks into the bungla, through the front door without knocking, ascends your stairs

unannounced, stands by the bed, wakes one
from sleep at midnight, taps once on the
shoulder, and says "Come." At dawn one is
fast in a coffin and feet deep beneath the sod,
and one's bungla and club know him or her
no more. And yet also in the East, life is so
easy and so pleasant, the attractions in the hour
so strong, the stimulus to all the senses so sharp,
that it seems perpetually to enjoin the lesson,
"Enjoy and heed not."

However, now I honestly meant to work hard
in the interests of the company. They should
have the best of my brains and my labours
through the winter. In the summer, according
to the agreement, I was free to return to
England, or, as I probably should do, to idle
my time away out there.

After my two hours' read, I got up and
stretched myself, took a turn round the room,
and then came up to lean my elbows on the
mantelpiece and stare absently in the glass. I
had a good deal more information to read up
in the next three weeks and each day was
precious. What a fool I had been to promise

A Man's Life

Digby to go to the Strongs' on Friday! To see this girl too! What was the good of that? Under any circumstances, merely to go and look at a woman is always waste of time.

Digby was a very tiresome fellow with women: not content with perpetually being in love with some impossible person himself, he seemed to derive a satisfaction from coming and pouring a description of her charms and beauties into my preoccupied ears, and finally, when assured of the hopelessness of his own cause, he would insist upon introducing me to her! I don't know quite what his idea was, nor what he thought he should gain if his goddesses smiled upon me, nor why he was always so confident that they would. I believe he honestly did think I was good-looking, but why? I asked myself, looking into the reflected face before me. I did not see much attractiveness in it myself: it was rather white and seedy-looking, with a blue shade about the eyes, which I said was due to overwork and liver, but which my friends unkindly ascribed to dissipation. I suppose it must have been the regularity of the

2

features and the straightness of the lines that gave me the title to be called decent-looking. Still, however flattering Digby's opinion of me might be, I could not feel in charity with him then. He had already, since I had come back to England, introduced me to two of his temporary deities—women with no possible attraction except their pretty, silly faces to recommend them, and I was not keen on seeing this latest wonder. Moreover, I was disinclined just then for English feminine talk and smiles, and the ways of English society bored me. I felt out of joint with life here altogether, just as my palate seemed out of taste with roast mutton after the curries of the East. I knew Mrs. Strong, the married sister of Theodora, slightly, through Digby, who was constantly at her house. She was a charming woman to speak to and charming to look at, and the leader of one of the most fashionable and fastest sets in town.

Of the sister I had not heard till now. Digby told me that when he first knew the Strongs the younger sister was in Paris, and it was only recently, at one of Mrs. Strong's receptions, that he had been introduced to her. I recalled idly what Digby had said of her. If his description were turned into more polished and artistic language, I saw that it might be the portrait of a beautiful and peculiar face. The former quality had little attraction, but I confess the latter had some. The new, the unusual, the unhabitual in everything possessed a great charm for me, and the more any object or any emotion deviated from the orthodox standard the greater the attraction it had for me. Still, at that time my work was paramount with me, and time valuable, and I concluded I had been a fool to say I would spare an evening even to see a curiosity. With this reflection I turned the gas out and went into bed.

CHAPTER II

IT was late when I reached the Strongs' on
Friday. I had been at work all day, and
had felt greatly disinclined to come at all;
should not have done so but that I had promised Digby. I had been disturbed by the
conflicting theories I had been reading as to
the worth of the latest excavations, and these
were drifting about in my mind as I walked
up the red carpeted steps into the hall. The
dancing had begun; in fact, I entered the
room in the middle of a waltz. The light
and movement helped me to pull myself together, and a faint feeling of interest began
to stir in me as I remembered I had to look
for a particular face. I took my stand by
the door where I had entered, at the end of
the room, and noted the couples as they came
down towards, and then passed, me. I knew
I must recognise Theodora by her peculiarity,

Six Chapters of a Man's Life

and I scanned the upper lip of all the girls who passed, but without result. I was beginning to think she could not be in the room, when my eyes were suddenly attracted, for no reason that I was conscious of, from the ring of dancers passing round the room to some in the centre. And there, coming down the middle of the room, under the full flood of light, was the face I was looking for. My attention was so riveted upon the face that I was not conscious of what figure belonged to it, nor did I see the shoulders that bore it. It might have been floating down towards me on the stream of light. What a face it was, too! White, so that it looked blanched under the pale, changeful, electric light, and lent a curious lustre by its gleaming, brilliant, swimming eyes. The mouth was a delicate curve of the brightest scarlet, and above, on the upper lip, was the sign I looked for, a narrow, glossy, black line. It was a handsome face of course, but that alone would not have excited my particular attention. One sees so many handsome faces. But such a tremendous

force of intellect sat on the brow, even amongst
the fashionably fuzzed curls, such a curious
fire shone in the scintillating eyes, and such
a peculiar half-male character invested the
whole countenance, that I felt violently attracted to it merely from its peculiarity. The
room round me seemed to vanish into a mere
whirl of chaotic light and colour, sound rose
and fell unheeded in the distance. That face
and I seemed left alone swimming in a sea
of light. It was only for a second, and then
I heard Digby's voice saying at my elbow in
an excited whisper:

"There she is! Now don't you think she's
a stunner? I can introduce you in a minute.
The waltz is just over."

"She is certainly handsome," I said quietly.
And I felt almost sorry, as she came up, that
I was going to be introduced. She is probably
in reality some silly *ingénue* like the rest, I
thought, with only two ideas in her head, and
those idiotic ones. The moment she speaks
the effect of her face will be spoiled.

As Digby murmured, "This is my friend,

14

A Man's Life

Mr. Cecil Ray," I noticed that she did not incline her head in the prescribed formal bow. Her eyes searched over my face, and an extra light seemed to flash from their pale, gleaming iris. Then I saw the vermilion bow of the mouth quiver and break up in a soft smile, and I heard her say—

"You've won your bet, Digby. I'll send you those cigars!"

Fast, I thought at once, in the hasty, unconsidered way one jumps to conclusions. But the voice was attractive; light in timbre, and one felt it would be capable of any number of inflections. I asked her if she could spare me a dance.

"Easily," she answered. "The present one, if you like."

"Would you like to dance, or are you tired?" I asked.

Now that she was close to me, I saw how delicate she looked, the effect of her white skin and the nervous, sensitive dilation of the eyes.

"I should like the rest," she said at once; "let's sit it out."

She laid her hand on my arm, and we turned into a sort of short corridor on our left, where there were some settees. It was lighted by stone statues with lamps in their hands, placed at intervals down it. She took her seat just under one of these, and I drew my settee up beside her. The light came straight down on her head from the lamp in the statue's hand—a statue of Bacchus—and I could not help thinking her face was rather like the one in stone above her. I did not trouble to speak. I just sat and watched her, and I waited with a mild curiosity to hear whether she would say anything worth listening to. There is an unquestionable charm in being in the society of people for whose opinion you don't care in the least— when you are absolutely indifferent as to what impression you produce. I felt no desire to please this girl, nor did I care whether she set me down as a perfect fool. I had come to see her, and she was certainly well worth seeing; but what she thought of me was not of the least consequence. It was too much trouble to talk the ordinary society twaddle, and I did not suppose she would understand or care for anything else; so I remained silent.

"Why do you keep looking up to this thing over my head?" she asked suddenly, catching my eyes.

"I was thinking how similar the face was to yours," I answered.

"What is it?" she asked, turning her head so that she could see it, and looking up to the nude figure, with its goat-skin on one shoulder and the vine twisted round its head.

"Oh, Dionysus! rather a disreputable individual to resemble."

"What do you know about Dionysus?" I asked with a laugh as she leaned back again.

"As much, I should think, and as little as anybody does."

"Have you had a classical training, then?" I asked in some surprise, looking at the beautiful, tight-laced, fashionable figure, the small, high-heeled shoes, and the fast-looking, artificial darkening of the eyes. She hardly looked like a votary of study. She nodded, as if not caring to pursue the subject.

"And who are your favourite authors?" I asked—"Martial and Aristophanes?"

I half thought that she would openly resent the veiled insult in my words, and I wanted to see her look indignant. Theodora however, only laughed.

"That means, I suppose, they are yours!" she answered. "I don't mind them. They have each said very perfect things, but I should not call them my favourites."

"And do you find nothing to condemn in ancient literature as a whole?" I said, looking at her.

A faint flush rose in either cheek, but the luminous, intelligent eyes met mine quite unconfused.

"Oh, I don't go in for condemning things. I read, and I see what the fellow has to say. I am not bound to agree. And then, of course, where I do not approve--well, *tout comprendre c'est tout pardonner;* and the same principle holds in life too."

I rather liked her for this last speech. She was evidently not the ordinary *ingénue,* and I felt vaguely interested.

18

A Man's Life

"But, independently of condemning, I suppose there are things you dislike—personally?"

"Oh, of course; yes, there is one thing I detest."

"What is it?"

"Priggishness."

I laughed, and so did she—a gay, high laugh that went echoing down the corridor.

There was silence for a minute or two, and then she said, "Would you like to smoke? You may, if you like. I don't mind."

"You smoke yourself?" I said.

"I do. Does that shock you? Some men think it fearful impropriety."

"I am not easily shocked, and I like——"

I was going to say impropriety, but I thought perhaps I was hardly justified, and I changed it to "unconventionality."

"Have you ever written anything?" I asked.

"No; it would be of no use with my laxity of opinions. I should only get bullyragged by all the reviewers; and I have no thirst for the 'glory that lives after men;' and in this present life—well, I have all."

A strikingly arrogant look came over the pale face, and I laughed.

"Take care!" I said. "As a classic scholar you certainly should be afraid to say such a thing. Just such a speech as to excite the φθόνος θεων."

The next minute I was sorry I had said the words, for she seemed to turn paler and shiver, and she answered impulsively, "Yes, I was wrong to say that; but, after all, the gods have no need to envy me. I am not at all happy. There is the one thing wanting in my life—the one thing to spoil all and guard me from the danger of too perfect good fortune. I am very lonely—I have no companion."

"And what would be the necessary qualifications for a man to have to attain that honour?" I said mockingly, catching her own cynical tone of a few minutes back. "For I suppose you don't contemplate a woman in the position?"

"Intellect," returned Theodora simply.

"Intellect!" I repeated, with my eyes on hers. "What do you want intellect in a man for?"

A Man's Life

I had gone just a little too far, possibly more in the tones than the words, or perhaps in the eyes that met hers.   She looked away from me and said coldly—

"That is an exceedingly rude remark."

"Not at all," I said, recovering myself. "You would have enough for both."

"Well turned," said Theodora with a laugh, and I felt she had forgiven me.

"And would looks have no influence with you?" I went on jestingly.

"Oh, yes," Theodora answered quietly, and not looking at me; "looks have a tremendous influence, but I don't think they are much good unless backed up by the sort of brain that happens to please one's own."

"Pray describe the particular sort that would be in your case," I said, watching her carefully under decorously drooped lids. She had a beautifully lined and planned figure—a form that any man would like to see expand and grow tense with passion for himself.

"Personally, I like some one who looks at everything from an entirely intellectual point

of view, who, in judging anything, has no bias
of any sort; such, I mean, as a religious person
or a moralist would have."

"Do you mean you have no religion and no
morality?" I asked, laughing outright.

Theodora looked at me distrustfully for a
second or two, and then said—

"I think we had better change the subject.
There is no good in telling you these things.
You will only talk them all over the place, and
while I am in this society it is easiest and
simplest to conform to its ways and never
mention personal views. I never do. I don't
know, I am sure, how we drifted into the
subject now."

"Because it is congenial to both of us," I
said hastily; "that must be it. Go on, I like
to hear you. I swear I won't repeat a word;
and as for myself, I have no religion and no
morals to boast of, so I am quite in with
you."

"What one feels," she answered lightly,
"with both religion and morality is that there
is no absoluteness about either. Both are

A Man's Life

merely—as, of course, has been said heaps of times—things of time and place; both vary directly with the latitude. How can one be either religious or moral all through one's life if one travels, for instance? Granted that in England I am a Christian, a very religious person—that is to say, I think as thirty millions of co-Christians think. I cross into India. There, amongst two hundred and fifty millions of Mahomedans and Hindus, I am most irreligious. Another example:—I am chaste and moral leaving the shores of Scotland, but I am profligate and abandoned when I touch the shore of Formosa. I have not altered, but Scot and Formosan do not agree on that most changeable of all fashions—virtue. And who is to say which is the better—Scot or Formosan? In one country it is enjoined by religion and morality to respect one's aged parents, in another to eat them. If I want to be religious and moral what am I to do, respect them or eat them? Or must I respect the one, say in England, in deference to one set of opinions, and eat the other in deference to another set in another country a few hundred miles off? Then too, a custom, polygamy say, for instance, highly fashionable and passing under the name of innocent pleasure with one nation, is abhorred as a crime by another. Millions call it the one, millions call it the other. How do you settle which it is? Why should I call it a crime here because others do, when, if I go into Turkey, I am told it is not a crime? What reason had I for saying it was a crime? Only because it was the fashion to say so? Very good. Then when I go elsewhere that reason is null. I condemned it because others did then; now, when I am in Turkey, am I to accept it because others do? Commit it merrily while I am here, and then pick up a holy horror and just loathing of it again when I move a few miles farther into a country where it is not in vogue? You would say, I suppose, 'Oh, well, you must pick up some religion and stick to it.' Very well, but then which, and why? All seem about upon a level: how can you decide which is better than the other? And if you admit they are all equal, then why take any particular man as a model? Why say I will think as Mahomet thought, and do as he directs; I will deny myself this and that because Christ, Mahomet, Buddha, Zoroaster, or Moses says one should? It seems so awfully funny."

I had listened to this in silence. It is delightful to hear one's own thoughts echoed suddenly in another's voice, to see them mirrored in another's brain, at least to me. "And so?" I said now, as she paused, "the conclusion?"

"Only, having all that in one's mind, the irreconcilability of creeds and morals prevents one caring about any. I have only one principle, I think, to guide me—to avoid inflicting injury on another. But as for vice, crime, sin, virtue, morality, belief, religion, they are all mere names to me."

"I thought you were an *ingénue*," I said, leaning forward and looking with a smile into the bright, clever face. "I need not have been afraid, need I?"

"You would probably have liked an *ingénue*

much better; most men do," she answered with a soft, sparkling smile.

"I don't," I said emphatically, looking down at the arm and hand from which she had drawn the glove as she talked, feeling instinctively certain that she as yet had no real knowledge of vice though she spoke so glibly of it.

What is that indefinable something in innocence that proclaims itself to a man? Like a subtle odour, like a faint current or a pale light diffused in the air of which one is but just conscious, it makes itself felt by us, and comes home to us, though we have no proof and no knowledge.

"And so, going back to where we started from, the question of companionship, it's most difficult," she continued. "I hate being with a person with whom I feel *genée*. It is dreadful to feel that one cannot say this, and must not say that, for fear of shocking their prejudices. It is such a bore. And then to listen to them is so irritating, when they talk of religion and this belief and that belief, when oneself has no belief; or to hear them referring to this moral

A Man's Life

law and that moral law for conduct and action, when one recognises none. It seems such nonsense. Just as if life were not hard enough and dreary enough without inventing tiresome restrictions and rules for oneself. So long as one acts honourably and steers clear of hurting anybody else, what can it matter what one does? That is why I admire the old Pagan religion so much. It enjoins nothing, forbids nothing; its only precept was—Enjoy."

"I don't think you feel very *genée* with me, do you?" I said.

"No; not at all. But still I fancy you don't think particularly well of me for what I have said," she answered.

"On the contrary," I said, growing serious, "I have liked all you have said. I know exactly what you mean. I have felt it myself often. A sort of restraint, a being *gené*, as you say. I thought I had contracted my looseness of morals in the East. I certainly feel more at home there now in every way than I do amongst English people—that is to say, generally," I added with a smile, and looked

27

at her. " I have felt delightfully at ease here to-night."

" Have you? I am so glad," she said impulsively, and then we were both silent. " I hate iconoclasts and puritans, and people like that old fool Wesley, don't you ? " she said, after a minute. " Fancy, I mean, destroying a statue simply because it was nude! That is the spirit I dislike so much. I should consider simply whether the thing were well executed of its kind or not, and if it were draped or un- draped, what does it matter ? Everything that helps to make life more pleasant, more beautiful, and more complex, I like. Laughter, and beauty, and art, and simplicity in nothing! To be simple, and humble, and moderate! the Christian virtues—good heavens! Just as if all the pleasure we can possibly get in life was not moderate enough ! "

I looked at the fugitive, scarlet tint in the pale cheeks, at the sweep of the thick eyelids over the scintillating eyes, and the line of the slight hip under her white silk skirt, and said in a low tone—

A Man's Life

" I think there may be some pleasures which are not so very moderate."

Her eyes rested on mine in rather a startled way for a second, and then a step came down the corridor. It broke in abruptly on us, and we both started and turned suddenly as if we had been found in a most compromising situation. We must have been sitting there some time; it was wonderful we had not been interrupted before.

" Your partner, I think, coming to claim you," I said as the figure came down the passage evidently to our seat. We both got up, and I took her hand as we stood by the statue of the god of licence and clasped it hard. It was a very curious hand, so extremely soft that as my fingers closed tighter and tighter over it, it seemed to yield and yield and collapse more and more like a piece of velvet within one's grasp. Where were its own bones and muscles, its own strength and will? I tried to find them by pressing it to my utmost, but it only sank, soft and burning, deeper into my palm, and lay there till I released it. As it

29

slid from me to her side again I felt vaguely that I was in the chains of a freshly-sprung passion. A dozen other men might clasp that hand in the evening unmoved and perceive no difference in it from any other; but in me the languid touch and the heat of the strengthless fingers seemed to appeal to every nerve in my own frame and excite them to response. Was not the hand an index to the whole form? I thought as my eyes glanced up the arm, rounded and supple and boneless, to the soft shoulder and the melting whiteness of the neck where I saw one pulse beat slowly. A sudden, dizzy longing to test it came over me, to draw the whole into my arms. Would not the whole figure, resistless and unresisting, lean, sink, melt into them, as the hand into my hand? Bah! Digby ought to be hanged for introducing me to her!

" Will you come and see me to-morrow? " and each word, as she said it, was like a caress.

" I shall be greatly honoured," I murmured, and we parted with a sense—and I think it was

A Man's Life

on either side—of an already greater intimacy than an hour's acquaintanceship justified. I went down the corridor, passing by the entrance to the rooms and out into the streets, and went back to my chambers. I took a turn up and down my rooms, thinking over what the girl had said, and above all of her personality. She was peculiar certainly in every way, and, contrary to the average Englishman, I liked peculiarity. And that intense nervous and physical excitability that I read in the dilated eyes enlisted my sympathies; perhaps because my own nerves always seemed strung to an unnatural pitch, like the overtuned strings of an instrument—the result partly, no doubt, of an irregular, ill-ordered life, and partly of fits of overwork, and principally of the organisation with which I had been cursed on entering the world. Cursed truly, for the phlegmatic fellow who goes through life without ever knowing he has a nervous system is the man to be envied. The rooms got too small and the atmosphere too oppressive after a time, and I turned out again to find my friend Thompson and get a

game of billiards out of him. It was four in
the morning when I returned, and then not to
sleep, merely to toss about and see everywhere
in the darkness of the room a charcoal-blackened
eye and a very white, slight, boneless arm.

CHAPTER III.

I DID not turn out of bed till ten o'clock the next morning, and I was still in dressing-gown and slippers, sitting by the fire looking over a map, when Digby came in upon me.

"Hullo, Ray, only just up, eh? as usual," was his first exclamation as he came in, his ulster buttoned up to his chin and the snow thick upon his boots. "What a fellow you are! I can't understand anybody lying in bed till ten o'clock in the morning."

"And I can't understand anybody driving up at seven," I said, smiling, and stirring my coffee idly. I had laid down the map with resignation. I knew Digby had come round to jaw for the next hour at least. "Can I offer you some breakfast?"

"Breakfast!" returned Digby, contemptuously. "No, thanks; I had mine hours ago. Well, what do you think of her?"

33

"Of whom? this Theodora?"

"Oh, it's Theodora already, is it?" said Digby, looking at me. "Well, never mind, go on. Yes, what do you think of her?"

"She seems rather clever, I think."

"Do you?" returned Digby, with a distinct accent of regret, as if I had told him I thought she squinted. "I never noticed it. But her looks, I mean."

"She is very peculiar," I said.

"But you like everything extraordinary; I should have thought that was just what would have attracted you."

"So it does," I admitted, "so much so that I am going to take the trouble of calling this afternoon expressly to see her again."

Digby stared hard at me for a minute, and then burst out laughing, "By Jove! you've made good use of your time. Did she ask you?"

"She did," I said.

"This looks as if it would be a case," remarked Digby lightly, and then added, "I'd have given anything to have had her myself,

34

but if it's not to be for me, I'd rather you be
the lucky one than any one else."

"Don't you think all that is a little
previous?" I said satirically, looking at him
over the coffee which stood on the maps of
Mesopotamia.

"Well, I don't know. You must marry
some time, Cecil."

"Really?" I said, raising my eyebrows and
regarding him with increased amusement.
"I think I have heard of men remaining
celibates before now, especially men with my
tastes."

"Yes," said Digby, becoming suddenly as
serious and thoughtful as if he were being
called upon to consider some weighty problem,
of which the solution must be found in the
next ten minutes. "I don't know how you
would agree. She is an awfully religious girl."

"Indeed?" I said, with a laugh; "how do
you know?"

Digby thought hard.

"She is," he said, with conviction at last.
"I see her at church every Sunday."

"Oh, then, of course she must be—proof
conclusive," I answered.

Digby looked at me, and then grumbled,
"Confounded sneering fellow you are. Has
she been telling you she is not?"

I remembered suddenly that I had promised
Theodora not to repeat her opinions, so I
only said, "I really don't know what she is;
she may be most devout for all I know—or
care."

"Of course, you can profess to be quite
indifferent," said Digby, ungraciously. "But
all I can say is, it doesn't look like it, your
going there this afternoon, and any way she
is not indifferent to you; she said all sorts of
flattering things about you."

"Very kind, I am sure," I murmured
derisively.

"And she sent round to my rooms this
morning a thundering box of Havanahs in
recognition of my having won the bet about
your looks."

I laughed outright.

"That's rather good 'biz' for you: the least

A Man's Life

you can do is to let me help in the smoking of them, I think."

"Of course I will; but it shows what she thinks of you, doesn't it?"

"Oh, most convincingly," I said with mock earnestness. "Havanahs are expensive things."

"But you know how awfully rich she is, don't you?" asked Digby, looking at me as if he wanted to find out whether I were really ignorant, or affecting to be so.

"My dear Charlie, you know I know nothing whatever about her except what you tell me; or do you suppose she showed me her banking account between the dances?"

"Don't know, I am sure," Digby grumbled back. "You sat in that passage long enough to be going through a banking account, and balancing it too, for that matter! However, the point is, she is rich—tons of money—over six thousand a year."

"Really?" I said, to say something.

"Yes; but she loses every penny on her marriage. Seems such a funny way to leave money to a girl, doesn't it? Some old pig of a maiden aunt tied it up in that way. Nasty thing to do, I think, don't you?"

"Very immoral of the old lady, it seems A girl like that, if she can't marry, will probably forego nothing but the ceremony."

"She runs the risk of losing her money though if anything were known; she only has it *dum casta manet,* just like a separation allowance."

"Hard lines," I murmured sympathetically.

"And so, of course, her people are anxious she should make a good match—take some man, I mean, with an income equal to what she has now of her own, so that she would not feel any loss. Otherwise, you see, if she married a poor man it would be rather a severe drop for her."

"Conditions calculated to prevent any fellow but a millionaire proposing to her, I should think," I said.

"Yes, except that she is a girl who does not care about money. She has been out now three seasons, and had one or two good chances and not taken them. Now myself, for instance, if

A Man's Life

she wanted money and position and so on, she could hardly do better, could she? And my family and the rest of it are all right. But she couldn't get over my red hair; I know it was that. She's mad upon looks. I know she is; she let it out to me once; and I bet you anything she'd take you and chuck over her money and everything else if you gave her the chance."

"I am certainly not likely to," I answered. "All this you have just told me alone would be enough to choke me off. I have always thought I could never love a decent woman unselfishly enough, even if she gave up nothing for me; and, great heavens, I should be sorry to value myself at—what do you say she has?—six thousand a year."

"Leave the woman who falls in love with the cut of your nose to do the valuation. You'll be surprised at the figure," said Digby with a touch of resentful bitterness, and getting up abruptly. "I'll look round in the evening," he added, buttoning up his overcoat. "Going to be in?"

"As far as I know," I answered, and he left.

Six Chapters of

I got up and dressed leisurely, thinking over
what he had said, and those words, "six thousand," repeating themselves unpleasantly in my
brain.

It was rather late for strict formality when I
found myself on the steps of her house. The
room I was shown into was large, much too
large to be comfortable on such a day, and I
had to thread my way through a perfect maze
of gilt-legged tables and statuette-bearing tripods
before I reached the hearth. Here burned a
small, quiet, chaste-looking fire, a sort of Vestal
flame, whose heat was lost upon the tessalated
tiles, white marble, and polished brass about it.
I stood looking down at it absently for a few
minutes, and then Theodora came in. She was
very simply dressed in some dark stuff that
fitted closely to her, and let me see the har-
monious lines of her figure as she came up to
me. The plain, small collar of the dress opened
at the neck, and from it a delicious, solid white
throat rose from the dull stuff like an almond
bursting from its husk. On the pale, well-cut
face and small head great care had evidently

been bestowed; the eyes were darkened, as last night, and the hair arranged with infinite pains on the forehead, and rolled into one massive glossy coil at the back.

She shook hands with a smile—a smile that failed to dispel the air of fatigue and fashionable dissipation which seemed to cling to her—and then wheeled a chair as near to the fender as she could get it. As she sat down I thought I had never seen such splendid shoulders combined with so slight a hip before.

"Now, I hope no one else will come to interrupt us," she said simply. "And don't let's bother to exchange comments on the weather nor last night's dance. I have done that six times over this morning with other callers. Don't let us talk for the sake of getting through a certain number of words. Let us talk because we are interested in what we are saying."

"I should be interested in anything if you said it," I answered.

"That's a fairly neat compliment," laughed Theodora. "Tell me something about the East, will you? That is a nice warm subject, and I feel so cold." And she shot out towards the blaze two well-made feet and ankles.

"Yes; in three weeks' time I shall be in a considerably warmer climate than this," I answered, drawing my chair as close to hers as fashion permits.

Theodora looked at me with a perceptibly startled expression as I spoke.

"Are you really going out so soon?" she said.

"I am really," I said with a smile.

"Oh, I am so sorry."

"Why?" I asked merely.

"Because I was thinking I should have the pleasure of meeting you lots more times at different functions."

"And would that be a pleasure?"

"Yes, very great," said Theodora, with a smile lighting her eyes and parting faintly the soft scarlet lips.

She looked at me, a seducing softness melting all her face and swimming in the liquid darkness of the eyes she raised to mine. A delicious intimacy seemed established between us by that

A Man's Life

smile; we seemed nearer to each other after it than before by many degrees. A month or two of time and ordinary intercourse may be balanced against the seconds of such a smile as this. A faint feeling of surprise mingled with my thoughts that she should show her own attitude of mind so clearly, but I believe she felt instinctively my attraction to her, and also undoubtedly she belonged to and had always been accustomed to a fast set. I was not the sort of man to find fault with her for that, and probably she had already been conscious of this, and felt all the more at ease with me. The opening primrose type of woman, the girl who does or wishes to suggest the modest violet unfolding beneath the rural hedge, had never had a charm for me. I do not profess to admire the simple violet; I infinitely prefer a well-trained hothouse gardenia. And this girl, about whom there was nothing of the humble, crooked-necked violet, in whom there was a dash of virility, a hint at dissipation, a suggestion of a certain decorous looseness of morals and fastness of manners, could stimulate me

43

with a keen sense of pleasure as our eyes or hands met.

"Why would it be a pleasure to meet me?" I asked, holding her eyes with mine, and wondering whether things would so turn out that I should ever kiss those parting lips before me.

Theodora laughed gently.

"For a good many reasons that it would make you too conceited to hear," she answered. "But one is because you are more interesting to talk to than the majority of people I meet every day. The castor of your chair has come upon my dress. Will you move it back a little, please?"

I pushed my chair back immediately and apologised.

"Are you going alone?" resumed Theodora.

"Quite alone."

"Is that nice?"

"No; I should have been very glad to find some nice fellow to go with me, but it's rather difficult. It is not everybody one meets that one would care to make such an exclusive companion of as a life like that out there necessitates. Still, there's no doubt I shall be dull, unless I can find some chum there."

"Some Englishman, I suppose?"

"Possibly; but they are mostly snobs who are out there."

Theodora made a faint sign of assent, and we both sat silent, staring into the fire.

"Does the heat suit you?" Theodora asked after a pause.

"Yes, I like it personally."

"So do I."

"I don't think any woman would like the climate I am going to now, or could stand it," I said.

Theodora said nothing; but I had my eyes on her face, which was towards the light of the fire, and I saw a tinge of mockery come over it. We had neither said anything further when the sound of a knock reached us, muffled owing to the distance the sound had to travel to reach us by the drawing-room fire at all, but distinct in the silence between us. Theodora looked at me sharply.

"There is somebody else. Do you want to leave yet ?" she said, and then added in a soft, persuasive tone, "Come into my own study, where we shan't be disturbed, and stay and have tea with me, will you ?"

She got up as she spoke: the room had darkened considerably while we had been sitting there, and only a dull light came from the leaden, snow-laden sky beyond the panes, but the firelight fell strongly across her figure as she stood, glancing and playing up it towards the slight waist and throwing scarlet upon the white throat and under part of the full chin. In the strong shadow on her face I could see merely the two seducing eyes. Easily excitable, where once a usually hypercritical, or rather hyperfanciful eye has been attracted, I felt a keen sense of pleasure stir me as I watched her rise and stand. That sense of pleasure which is nothing more than an assurance to the roused and unquiet instincts within one, of future satisfaction or gratification, with, from, or at the expense of the object creating the sensation. Unconsciously a certainty of

46

A Man's Life

possession of Theodora to-day, to-morrow, or next year, filled me for the moment as completely as if I had just made her my wife. The instinct that demanded her was immediately answered by a mechanical process of the brain, not with doubt or fear but simple confidence: this is a pleasant and delightful object to you, as others have been; later, it will be a source of enjoyment to you, as others have been. And the lulling of this painful instinct is what we know as pleasure. And this instinct and its answer is exactly that which we should not feel within us for any beloved object: it is this that tends inevitably to degrade the loved one and debase our own passion. If the object is worthy and lovely in any sense, we should be ready to love it as being such, for itself, as moralists preach to us of Virtue, as theologians preach to us of the Deity. To love, or at least to strive to love, an object for the object's sake, and not our own sake, to love it in its relation to its pleasure and not in its relation to our own pleasure, is to feel the only love which is worthy of offering to a fellow human being, the one which elevates—and the only one— both giver and receiver. If we ever learn this lesson, we learn it late. I had not learned it yet.

I murmured a prescribed "I shall be delighted," and followed Theodora behind a huge red tapestry screen that reached half-way up to the ceiling. We were then face to face with a door which she opened, and we both passed over the threshold together. She had called the room her own, so I glanced round it with a certain curiosity. A room is always some faint index to the character of its occupier, and as I looked, a smile came to my face: it suggested everywhere, as I should have expected, an intellectual but careless and dissolute mind. There were two or three tables in the window heaped up with books and strewn over with papers. The centre table had been pushed away to leave a clearer space by the grate, and an arm-chair, seemingly of unfathomable depths, and a sofa dragged forward in its place. Within the grate roared a tremendous fire, banked up

48

A Man's Life

half-way to the chimney, and a short poker was
thrust into it between the bars: the red light
leaped over the whole room and made it
brilliant, and glanced over a rug and some
tumbled cushions on the floor in front of the
fender, evidently where she had been lying.
Now, however, she picked up the cushions and
tossed them into the corner of the couch and
sat down herself in the other corner.

"Do you prefer the floor generally?" I said,
sitting down in the arm-chair as she indicated it
to me.

"Yes, one feels quite free and at ease lying
on the floor, whereas on a couch its limits are
narrow, and one has the constraint and bother
of taking care one does not go to sleep and roll
off."

"But suppose you did, you would then but
be upon the floor."

"Quite so, but I should have the pain of
falling." Our eyes met each other's across the
red flare of the firelight.

Theodora went on jestingly, "Now these are
the ethics of the couch and the floor: I lay

myself voluntarily upon the floor, knowing it thoroughly as a trifle low but undeceptive, suitable to the condition of sleep, which will probably arise, and suitable to my requirements of ease and space; I avoid the restricted and uncertain couch, recognising that if I fall to sleep on that raised level and the desire to stretch myself should come, I shall awake with pain and shock to feel the ground and see above me the couch from which I fell—see?" She spoke lightly and with a smile, and I listened with one; but her eyes told me that these ethics of the couch and floor covered the ethics of life. " No, you must accept the necessity of the floor, I think, unless you like to forego your sleep and have the trouble of taking care to stick upon your couch; and for me, the difference of level between the two is not worth the additional bother." She laughed and I joined her. " What do you think ? " she asked.

I looked at her as she sat opposite me, the firelight playing all over her, from the turn of her knee just marked beneath her skirt to her splendid shoulders and the smooth, soft hand

and wrist supporting the distinguished little
head. I did not tell her what I was thinking.
What I said was, "You're very logical: I am
quite convinced there's no place like the ground
for a siesta."

Theodora laughed and laid her hand on the
bell. A second or two after, a door, other than
the one we had entered by, opened and a maid
appeared.

"Bring tea and pegs," said Theodora, and
the door shut again. "I ordered pegs for you,
because I know men hate tea," she said. "That's
my own maid. I never let any of the servants
answer this bell except her: she has my confidence as far as one ever gives confidence to a
servant. I think she likes me: I like making
myself loved," she added impulsively.

"You've never found the least difficulty in it,
I should think," I answered, perhaps a shade
more warmly than I ought, for the colour came
into her cheek and a slight confusion into her
eyes. The servant's re-entry saved her from
replying.

"Now, tell me how you like your peg made,

and I'll make it," said Theodora, getting up and crossing to the table when the servant had gone. I got up too, and protested against this arrangement. Theodora turned round and looked up at me, leaning one hand on the table.

"Now, how ridiculous and conventional you are!" she said. "You would think nothing of letting me make you a cup of tea, and yet I must by no means mix you a peg!"

She looked so like a young fellow of nineteen or so as she spoke, that half the sense of informality between us was lost, and there was a keen, subtle pleasure in this superficial familiarity with her that I had never felt with far prettier women. The half of nearly every desire is curiosity, a vague, undefined curiosity, of which we are hardly conscious, and it was this that Theodora so violently stimulated, while her beauty was sufficient to nurse the other half. This feeling of curiosity arises, of course, for any woman who may be new to us, and who has the power to move us at all, but generally, if it cannot be gratified for the particular one, it is more or less satisfied by the

A Man's Life

general knowledge applying to them all; but here, as Theodora differed so much from the ordinary feminine type, even this instinctive consolation was denied me. I looked down at her with a smile.

"We shan't be able to reconcile Fashion and Logic, so it's no use," I said. "Make the peg, then, and I'll try and remain in the fashion by assuming it's tea."

"Great Scott! I hope you won't fancy it's tea while you are drinking it!" returned Theodora, laughing.

She handed me the glass, and I declared nectar wasn't in it with that peg; and then she made her own tea and came and sat down to drink it in not at all an indecorous, but still informal proximity.

"Did you collect anything in the East?" she asked me after a minute or two.

"Yes, a good many idols and relics and curiosities of sorts," I answered. "Would you like to see them?"

"Very much," Theodora answered. "Where are they?"

"Well, not in my pocket," I said, smiling; "at my chambers. Could you and Mrs. Strong spare an afternoon and honour me with a visit there?"

"I should like it immensely. I know Hester will come if I ask her."

"When you have seen them I must pack them up and send them to my agents. One can't travel about with those things."

A sort of tremor passed over Theodora's face as I spoke, and her glance met mine, full of demands and questionings and a very distinct assertion of distress; it said distinctly, "I am so sorry you are going." The sorrow in her eyes touched my vanity deeply, which is the most responsive quality we have. It is difficult to reach our hearts or our sympathies, but our vanity is always available. I felt inclined to throw my arm round that supple-looking waist —and it was close to me—and say, "Don't be sorry. Come too." I don't know whether my looks were as plain as hers, but Theodora rose carelessly, apparently to set her tea-cup down, and then did not resume her seat by me, but

54

A Man's Life

went back to the sofa on the other side of the rug. This, in the state of feeling into which I had drifted, produced an irritated sensation, and I was rather pleased than not when a gong sounded somewhere in the house and gave me a graceful opening to rise.

"May I hope to hear from you, then, which day you will like to come?" I said, as I held out my hand.

Now this was the moment I had been expecting practically ever since her hand left mine, the moment when it should touch it again—I do not mean consciously; but there are a million slight, vague physical experiences and sensations within us of which the mind remains unconscious. Theodora's white right hand rested on her hip, the light from above struck upon it, and I noted that all the rings had been stripped from it: her left was crowded with them, so that the hand sparkled at each movement, but not one remained on her right. I coloured violently for the minute as I recollected my last night's pressure, and the idea flashed upon me at once that she had removed them expressly to avoid the pain of having them ground into her flesh. The next second Theodora had laid her hand confidently in mine. My mind, annoyed at the thought just shot through it, bade me take it loosely and let it go; but Theodora raised her eyes to me full of a soft disappointment, which seemed to say, "Are you not going to press it then, after all, when I have taken off all the rings entirely that you may ?" That look seemed to push away, walk over, ignore my reason and appeal directly to the eager physical nerves and muscles. Spontaneously, whether I would or not, they responded to it, and my fingers laced themselves tightly round this morsel of velvet-covered fire. We forgot in those few seconds to say the orthodox good-byes, she forgot to answer my question: what we both were saying to each other, though our lips did not open, was—

"*So* I should like to hold and embrace you," and she, "*So* I should like to be held and embraced." Then she withdrew her hand, and I went out by way of the drawing-room, where we had entered. In the hall her footmen

A Man's Life

showed me out with extra obsequiousness: my three hours' stay raised me, I suppose, to the rank of more than an ordinary caller.

It was dark now in the streets, and the temperature must have been somewhere about zero. I turned my collar up, and started to walk sharply in the direction of my chambers. Walking always induces in me a tendency to reflection and retrospection ; and now, removed from the excitement of Theodora's actual presence, my thoughts lapped quietly over the whole interview, going through it backwards, like the calming waves of a receding tide leaving lingeringly the sand. There was no doubt that this girl attracted me very strongly ; that the passion born yesterday was nearing adolescence; and there was no doubt, too, that I ought to strangle it now before it reached maturity. My thoughts, however, turned impatiently from this question, and kept closing and centring round the object itself with maddening persistency. I laughed to myself as Schopenhauer's theory shot across me, that all impulse to love is merely the impulse of the genius of the genus to select a fitting object which will help in producing the Third Life. Certainly the genius of the genus in me was weaker than the genius of my own individuality here, for Theodora was as unfitted, according to the philosopher's views, to become a co-worker with me in carrying out nature's sole aim as she was fitted to give me as an individual the strongest personal pleasure.

It may be, granted that the first moving of desire in a lover is the mere striving of Nature to produce the Third Life, and that she leads him unconsciously to desire an object most suited to the requirements of the future being, rather than his own; granted that in many men nature is powerful to this extent, it may be that in others, the demands and stimulus of the mind strangle the instincts of nature, and wilfully force the lover towards some object where the aims of nature may not be seconded, may even be defeated, but where the will and the desire of the individual will receive its greatest possible gratification.

A Man's Life

I remember Schopenhauer does admit that this instinct in man is apt to be led astray; and it is fortunate he did not forget to make this admission, if his theory is to be generally applied, considering how very particularly often we are led astray, and that our strongest, fiercest passions and keenest pleasures are constantly not those suitable to or in accordance with the ends of nature. It has always seemed to me that the sharpest, most violent stimulus—we may say the true essence of pleasure—lies in some gratification which has no claim whatever in any sense to be beneficial or useful, or have any ulterior motive, conscious or instinctive, or any lasting result, or any fulfilment of any object, but which is simple gratification, and dies naturally in its own excess.

As we admit of works of pure genius that they cannot claim for themselves utility or motive or purpose, but simply that they exist as joy-giving and beautiful objects of delight, so must we have done with utility, motive, purpose, and the aims of nature before we can reach the most absolute degree of positive pleasure.

To choose an ordinary, simple, admissible instance: A naturally hungry man, given a slice of bread, will he or will he not devour it with as great a pleasure as the craving drunkard feels in swallowing a draught of raw brandy?

In the first case a simple, natural desire is gratified, and the aim of nature satisfied; but the individual's longing and subsequent pleasure cannot be said to equal the furious crave of the drunkard, and his delirious sense of gratification as the brandy burns his throat.

This inclination towards Theodora could hardly be the simple, natural instinct, guided by natural selection; for then, surely, I should have been swayed towards some more womanly individual, some more vigorous and, at the same time, more feminine physique. No; it was the mind that had first suggested to the senses, and the senses that had answered in a dizzy pleasure, that this passionate, sensitive frame, with its tensely strung nerves and excitable pulses, promised the height of satisfaction to a lover; but surely to Nature it promised

A Man's Life

a poor, if possible, mother, and a still poorer
nurse. And these desires and passions, which
spring from that borderland between mind and
senses, and are nourished by the suggestions of
the one and the stimulus of the other, have a
strong grip upon our organisation, because they
offer an acuter pleasure than those simple and
purely physical ones in which Nature is striving
after her own ends, and using us simply as her
instruments. I thought on in a desultory sort
of way, more or less about Theodora, and
mostly about the state of my own feelings,
until I reached my chambers. There I found
Digby, and in his society, with his chaff and
gabble in my ears, all philosophy and reflection
fled, without leaving me any definite decision
made.

The next afternoon but one found myself
and Digby standing at the window of my
chambers awaiting Theodora's arrival. I had
invited him to help me entertain the two
women, and also help me unearth and dust
my store of idols and curiosities and range
them on the tables for inspection. There were

61

crowds of knick-knacks picked up in the crooked streets and odd corners of Benares, trifles bought in the Cairo bazaars, and vases and coins discovered below the soil in the regions of the Tigris. Concerning several of the most typical objects Digby and I had had considerable difference of opinion. One highly interesting bronze model of the monkey-god at Benares he had declared I could not exhibit on account of its too pronounced realism and insufficient attention to the sartorial art. I had declared that the god's deficiencies in this respect were not more pronounced than the objects in flesh tints, hung at the Academy, that Theodora viewed every season.

" Perhaps not," he had answered. " But this is *not* in pink and white and hung on the Academy walls for the public to stare at, and therefore you can't let her see it."

This was unanswerable. I yielded, and the monkey-god was wheeled under a side-table, out of view. Every shelf, and stand, and table had been pressed into the service, and my rooms had the appearance of a corner in an

A Man's Life

Egyptian bazaar now when we had finished our preparations.

"There they are," said Digby, as Mrs. Strong's victoria came in sight.

Theodora was leaning back beside her sister, and it struck me then how representative she looked as it were of herself and her position. From where we stood we could see down into the victoria as it drew up at our door. Her knees were crossed under the blue carriage rug, on the edge of which rested her two small pale-gloved hands. A velvet jacket that fitted her as its skin fits the grape showed us her magnificent shoulders and the long easy slope of her figure to the small waist. On her head, in the least turn of which lay the acme of distinction, amongst the black glossy masses of her hair, sat a small hat in vermilion velvet, made to somewhat resemble the Turkish fez. As the carriage stopped she glanced up, and a brilliant smile swept over her face as she bowed slightly to us at the window. The handsome, painted eyes, the naturally scarlet lips, the pallor of the oval face, and each

well-trained movement of the distinguished
figure as she rose and stepped from the
carriage, was noted and watched by our four
critical eyes.

"A typical product of our nineteenth century
civilisation," I said with a faint smile, as
Theodora let her fur-edged skirt draw over
the snowy pavement, and we heard her clear,
cultivated tones, with the fashionable drag in
them, ordering the coachman not to let the
horses get cold.

"But she's a splendid sort of creature, don't
you think?" said Digby. "Happy the man
who—— eh?"

I nodded.

"Yes," I assented, "but how much that man
should have to offer, old chap; that's the point.
That six thousand of hers seems an invulnerable
protection."

"I suppose so," said Digby with a nervous
yawn. "And to think I have more than
double that, and yet—— It's a pity. Funny
it will be if my looks and your poverty prevent
either of us having her."

A Man's Life

" My own case is settled," I said decisively. " My position and hers decide it for me."

" I'd change places with you this minute if I could," muttered Digby moodily, as steps came down to our door and we went forward to meet the women as they entered.

It seemed to arrange itself naturally that Digby should be occupied in the first few seconds with Mrs. Strong, and that I should be free to receive Theodora.

Of all the lesser emotions there is hardly any one greater than that subtle sense of pleasure felt when the woman we love crosses for the first time our own threshold. We may have met her a hundred times in her house or on public ground, but the sensation her presence then creates is altogether different from that instinctive, involuntary, momentary, and delightful sense of ownership which rises when she enters any room essentially our own. It is the very illusion of possession. With this hatefully egoistic satisfaction infused through me, I drew forward for her my own favourite chair and Theodora sank into it, and her tiny, exquisitely formed feet sought my fender rail. At a murmured invitation from me she unfastened and laid aside her cloak. Beneath, she revealed some purplish silk-like material that seemed shot with different colours as the firelight fell upon it; it was strained tight and smooth upon her, and the swell of a low bosom was distinctly defined below it. There was no excessive development, quite the contrary, but in the very slightness there was an indescribably sensuous curve, and a depression rising and falling that seemed as if it might be the very home itself of passion. It was a breast with little suggestion of the duties or powers of nature, but with infinite seduction for a lover.

"What a marvellous collection you have here!" she said, throwing a glance round the room. "What made you bring home all these things?"

"The majority were gifts to me—presents made by the different natives whom I visited or came into connection with in various ways. A native is never happy, if he likes you at all, until he has made you some valuable present."

A Man's Life

"You must be very popular with them, indeed," returned Theodora, glancing from a
brilliant Persian carpet suspended on the wall
to a gold and ivory model of a temple on the
console by her side.

"Well, when one stays with a fellow as his
guest, as I have done with some of these small
rajahs and people, of course one tries to make
oneself agreeable."

"The fact is, Miss Dudley," interrupted
Digby, "Rays admires these fellows, and that
is why they like him. Just look at this sketch-
book of his—what trouble he has taken to
make portraits of them," and he stretched out
a limp-covered pocket album of mine. I red-
dened slightly, and tried to intercept his hand.

"Nonsense, Digby; give the book to me," I
said, but Theodora had already taken it, and
she looked at me as I spoke with one of those
delicious looks that could speak so clearly; now
it seemed to say, "If you are going to love me,
you must have no secrets from me."

She opened the book, and I was subdued
and let her. I did not much care, except that

it was some time now since I had looked at it,
and I did not know what she might find in it:
however, Theodora was so different from girls
generally, that it did not greatly matter.

" Perhaps these are portraits of your different
conquests amongst the ranees, are they?" she
said. " I don't see 'My Victims,' though,
written across the outside, as the Frenchmen
write on their albums."

"No," I said with a smile; "I think these
are only portraits of men whose appearance
struck me, or with whom I had some friendship. The great difficulty is to get any
Mahomedan to let you draw him."

The very first leaf she turned seemed to give
the lie to my words. Against a background of
yellow sand and blue sky stood out a slight figure
in white bending a little backward and holding
in its hands, extended on either side, the
masses of its black hair that fell through them
till they touched the sand by its feet. Theodora threw a side glance full of derision on me
as she raised her eyes from the page.

" I swear it isn't," I said hastily, colouring,
68

A Man's Life

for I saw she thought it was a woman. "It's a young Sikh I bribed to let me paint him."

"Oh, a young Sikh, is it?" said Theodora, bending over the book again. "Well, it is a lovely face, and what beautiful hair!"

"Yes, almost as beautiful as yours," I murmured in safety, for the others were wholly occupied in testing the limits of the flexibility of the soap stone. Not for any consideration in this world could I have restrained the irresistible desire to say the words, looking at her, sitting sideways to me, noting that shining weight of hair lying on the white neck, and that curious masculine shade upon the upper lip. A faint liquid smile came to her face.

"Mine is not so long as that, when you see it undone," she said, looking at me.

"How long is it?" I asked, mechanically turning over the leaves of the sketch-book and thinking in a crazy sort of way what I would not give to see her in intimate informality, with that hair unloosed, and have the right to lift a single strand of it.

69

"It would not touch the ground," she answered. "It must be about eight inches off it, I think."

"A marvellous length for a European," I answered in a conventional tone, though it was a difficulty to summon it. Within my brain all the dizzy thoughts seemed reeling together till they left me hardly conscious of anything but an acute, painful sense of her proximity.

"Find me the head of a Persian, will you?" came her voice next.

"A Persian?" I repeated mechanically.

Theodora looked at me wonderingly, and I recalled myself.

"Oh yes, I'll find you one. Give me the book."

I took the book and turned over the leaves towards the end. As I did so some of the intermediate pages caught her eye, and she tried to arrest the turning leaves.

"What is that? Let me see."

"It is nothing," I said, passing them over. "Allow me to find you the one you want."

Theodora did not insist, but her glance said,

A Man's Life.

"I will be revenged for this resistance to my wishes."

When I had found her the portrait I laid the open book back upon her knees. Theodora bent over it with an unaffected exclamation of delight. "How exquisite! and how well you have done it! What a talent you must have!"

"Oh no, no talent," I said hastily. "It's easy to do a thing like that when your heart is in it."

Theodora looked up at me and said simply, "This is a woman;" and I looked back in her eyes and said as simply, "Yes, it is a woman."

Theodora was silent, gazing at the open leaf, absorbed; and half unconsciously my eyes followed hers, and rested with hers on the page. Many months had gone by since I had opened the book, and many, many cigars, that, according to Tolstoy, deaden every mental feeling, and many, many pints of brandy, that do the same thing—only more so—had been consumed since I had last looked upon that face. And now I saw it over the shoulder of this woman. And the old pain revived and surged through

me, but it was dull, dull, as every emotion must
be in the near neighbourhood of a new object of
desire—every emotion except one.

"Really it is a very beautiful face, isn't it?"
she said at last with a tender and sympathetic
accent, and as she raised her head our eyes met.

I looked at her and answered, "I should say
'Yes' if we were not looking at it together;
but, you know, beauty is entirely a question of
comparison."

Her face was not one-tenth so handsome as
the mere shadowed inanimate representation of
the Persian's beneath our hands. I knew it,
and so did she. Theodora herself would have
been the first to admit it. But nevertheless the
words were ethically true,—true in the sense
that underlay the society compliment, for no
beauty of the dead can compare with that of
the living. Such are we that as we love all
objects in their relation to our own pleasure
from them, so even in our admiration the
greatest beauty, when absolutely useless to us,
cannot move us as a far lesser degree has the
power to do, from which it is possible to hope,

A Man's Life

however vaguely, for some personal gratification. And to this my words would come if translated, and I think Theodora understood the translation rather than the conventional form of them, for she did not take the trouble to deprecate the flattery.

I got up, and to change the subject, said, "Let me wheel up that little table of idols; some of them are rather curious."

I moved the tripod up to the arm of her chair. Theodora closed the sketch-book and put it beside her, and looked over the miniature bronze gods with interest. Then she stretched out her arm to lift and move several of them, and her soft fingers seemed to lie caressingly— as they did on everything they touched—on the heads and shoulders of the images. I watched her, envying those senseless little blocks of brass.

"This is the Hindu equivalent of the Greek Aphrodite," I said, lifting forward a small, un-utterably hideous, squat female figure, with the face of a monkey, and two closed wings of a dragon on its shoulders.

"Oh, Venus!" said Theodora; "we must certainly crown her amongst them, though hardly, I think, in this particular case for her beauty." And she laughingly slipped off a diamond half-hoop from her middle finger and slipped the ring on to the model's head. It fitted exactly round the repulsive brows of the deformed and stunted image, and the goddess stood crowned in the centre of the table amongst the other figures with the circlet of brilliants flashing brightly in the firelight on her head.

As Theodora passed the ring from her own warm white finger on to the forehead of the misshapen idol, she looked at me. The look, coupled with the action, in my state, went home to those very inner cells of the brain where are the springs themselves of passion. At the same instant the laughter and irresponsible gaiety and light pleasure on the face before me, the contrast between the delicate hand and the repellent monstrosity she had crowned—the sinister allegorical significance struck me like a blow. An unexplained feeling of rage filled me—was it

A Man's Life

against her, myself, her action, or my own desires? It seemed for the moment to burn against them all. On the spur of it I dragged forward to myself another of the images from behind the Astarte, slipped off my own signet ring, and put it on the head of the idol.

"This is the only one for me to crown!" I said bitterly with a laugh, feeling myself whiten with the stress and strain of a host of inexplicable sensations that crowded in upon me as I met Theodora's lovely, inquiring glance.

There was a shadow of apprehensiveness in her voice as she said, "What is that one?"

"Shiva," I said curtly, looking her straight in the eyes. "The god of self-denial."

I saw the colour die suddenly out of her face, and I knew I had hurt her; but I could not help it. With her glance she had summoned me to approve or second her jesting act. It was a challenge I could not pass over. I must in some correspondingly joking way either accept or reject her coronation. And to reject it was all I could do, since this woman must be nothing to me. There was a second's blank pause of strained silence, but superficially we had not strayed off the legitimate ground of mere society nothings, whatever we might feel underlay them, and Theodora was trained thoroughly in the ways of fashion.

The next second she leaned back in her chair, saying lightly, "A false, absurd, and unnatural god. It is the greatest error to strive after the impossible, it merely prevents you accomplishing the possible. Gods like these," and she indicated the abominable, squint-eyed Venus, "are merely natural instincts personified, and one may well call them gods, since they are invincible. Don't you remember the fearful punishments that the Greeks represented as overtaking mortals who dared to resist nature's laws that they chose to individualise as their gods? You remember the fate of Hypolitus who tried to disdain Venus, of Pentheus who tried to subdue Bacchus? Those two plays teach the immortal lesson that if you have the presumption to try to be greater than Nature, she will in the end take a terrible revenge. The most we can do is to guide her.

A Man's Life

You can never, never be her conqueror. Consider yourself fortunate if she allows you to be
her charioteer."

It was all said very lightly and jestingly, but
at the last phrase there was a flash in her eyes
directed upon me—yes, me—as if she read
down into my inner soul, and it sent the blood
to my face. As the last word left her lips she
stretched out her hand and deliberately took
my ring from the head of Shiva, put it above
her own diamonds on the other idol, and laid
the god I had chosen—the god of austerity and
mortification—prostrate on its face at the feet
of the leering Venus. Then without troubling
to find a transition phrase, she got up and
said, " I am going to look at that Persian
carpet."

It had all taken but a few seconds; the next
minute we were over by the carpet, standing in
front of it and admiring its hues in the most
orthodox terms. The images were left as she
had placed them; I could do nothing less,
of course, than yield to a woman—and my
guest.

Six Chapters of

The jest had not gone towards calming my feelings; nor had those two glances of hers, the first so tender and appealing, so feminine, as she had crowned the Venus, the second so virile and scornful, as she had discrowned the Shiva. There was a strange mingling of extremes in her: at one moment she seemed will-less, deliciously weak, a thing only made to be taken in one's arms and kissed; the next, she was full of independent, uncontrollable determination and opinion.

Most men would have found it hard to be indifferent to her. When beside her you must either have been attracted or repelled. For me, she was the very worst woman that could have crossed my path. I disliked in a mild, theoretical way, women in the general term. I had an aversion, slight and faint it is true, but still an aversion, to everything suggestively, typically feminine; but Theodora, with her peculiarity, her apparent power of mind, her hermaphroditism of looks, stimulated violently that strongest, perhaps, of our feelings—curiosity. As I stood beside her now, her shoulder only a little below my own, her neck and the line of her breast just visible to the side vision of my eyes, and heard her talking of the carpet, I felt there was no price I would not have paid to have stood for one half-hour in intimate confidence with her and been able to tear the veils from this irritating personality.

From the carpet we passed on to a table of Cashmere work, and next, to a pile of Mahomedan garments. These had been packed with my own personal luggage. It was Digby who, having seen them by chance, had insisted that they would add interest to the general collection of Eastern trifles.

"Clothes, my dear fellow, clothes. Why, they will probably please her more than anything else."

Theodora advanced to the heap of stuffs and lifted one of them.

"What is the history of these?" she said, laughing. "These were not presents to you."

"No," I murmured; "bought in the different bazaars."

"Some, perhaps," returned Theodora, throwing her glance over them; "but a great many are not new."

It struck me she would not be a woman very easy to deceive. Some men value a woman in proportion to the ease with which they can impose upon her; but it is too much trouble to me to deceive at all, so that the absence of that amiable quality did not disquiet me. On the contrary, the comprehensive, cynical, and at the same time indulgent smile that came so readily to Theodora's lips charmed me more, because it was the promise of even less trouble than a real or professed obtuseness.

"No," I assented merely.

"Well, then?" asked Theodora, but without troubling to seek a reply. "How pretty they are, and how curious! this one, for instance," and she took up a blue silk Zouave jacket, covered with gold embroidery, and worth perhaps about thirty pounds. "This has been a good deal worn; it is a souvenir, I suppose?"

I nodded. With any other woman I was similarly anxious to please I should have denied it—but with her, I felt it did not matter.

A Man's Life

"Too sacred, then, perhaps for me to put on," she said, with her hand in the collar, and smiling derisively.

"Oh dear no," I said, "not at all. Put it on, by all means."

"Nothing is sacred to you, eh? I see; hold it then."

She gave me the *Zouave* and turned for me to put it on. A glimpse of the back of her white neck as she bent her head forward, a convulsion of those adorable shoulders as she drew on the jacket, and the *Zouave* was fitted on; two seconds, perhaps, but my self-control wrapped round me had lost one of its skins.

"Now I must find a turban or fez," she said, turning over gently but without any ceremony the pile; "oh, here's one." She drew out a white fez, also embroidered in gold, and removing her hat, put it on very much to one side, amongst her black hair, and then affecting an undulating gait, she walked over to the fire.

"How do you like me in Eastern dress, Hester?" she said, addressing her sister, for whom Digby was deciphering some old coins.

Digby and I confessed afterwards to each other the impulse that moved us both to suggest it was not at all complete without the trousers. I did offer her a cigarette to enhance the effect.

"Quite passable, really," said Mrs. Strong, leaning back and surveying her languidly.

Theodora took the cigarette with a laugh, lighted and smoked it; and it was then, as she leaned against the mantelpiece with her eyes full of laughter, a glow on her pale skin, and an indolent relaxation in the long supple figure, that I first said—or rather an involuntary, unrecognised voice within me said, "It is no good; whatever happens, I must have you."

"Do you know that it is past six, Theo?" said Mrs. Strong.

"You will let me give you a cup of tea before you go," I said.

"Tea!" repeated Theodora; "I thought you were going to say haschisch, or opium at the least, after such an Indian afternoon."

"I have both," I answered; "would you

like some?" thinking, "By Jove, I should like to see you after the haschisch."

"No," replied Theodora; "I make it a rule not to get intoxicated in public."

When the women rose to go, Theodora, to my regret, divested herself of the *Zouave* without my aid, and declined it also for putting on her own cloak.

As they stood drawing on their gloves, I asked if there was anything they thought worthy of their acceptance amongst these curiosities. Mrs. Strong chose from the table near her an ivory model of the Taj, and Digby took it up to carry for her to the door. As he did so his eye caught the table of images.

"This is your ring, Miss Dudley, I believe," he said.

I saw him grin horridly as he noted the arrangement of the figures — doubtless he thought it was mine.

I took up my signet ring again, and Theodora said carelessly, without the faintest tinge of colour rising in her cheek, "Oh yes, I had forgotten it—thanks."

She took it from him, and replaced it.

I asked her if she would honour me, as her sister had done.

"There is one thing in this room I covet immensely," she said, meeting my gaze.

"It is yours then, of course," I answered. "What is it?"

Theodora stretched out her open hand.

"Your sketch-book."

For a second I felt the blood suddenly dye all my face. The request took me by surprise for one thing, and immediately after the surprise followed the vexatious and embarrassing thought that she had asked for the one thing in the rooms that I did not certainly wish her to have. The book contained a hundred memories, embodied in writing, sketching, and painting, of those six years in the East. There was not a page in it that did not reflect the emotions of the time when it had been filled in, and give a chronicle of the life lived at the date inscribed on it. It was a sort of diary in cipher, and to turn over its leaves was to re-live the hours they represented. For my

A Man's Life

own personal pleasure I liked the book and wanted to keep it, but there were other reasons too why I disliked the idea of surrendering it. It flashed through me the question as to what her object was in possessing herself of it. Was it jealousy of the faces or any face within it that prompted her? and would she amuse herself, when she had it, by tearing out the leaves or burning it? To give over the portraits merely to be sacrificed to a petty feminine spite and malice jarred upon me. Involuntarily I looked hard into her eyes to try and read her intentions, and I felt I had wronged her. The eyes were full of the softest, tenderest light, it was impossible to imagine them vindictive. She had seen my hesitation, and she smiled faintly.

"Poor Herod, with your daughter of Herodias," she said softly. "Never mind, I will not take it."

The others, who had been standing with her, saw there was some embarrassment that they did not understand, and Mrs. Strong turned to go slowly down the corridor. Digby had to follow. Theodora was left standing alone before me, her seductive figure framed in the open doorway. Of course, she was irresistible: was she not the new object of my desires? I seized the sketch-book from the chair. What did anything matter?

"Yes," I said, hastily putting it into that soft, small hand before it could draw back. "Forgive me the hesitation. You know I would give you anything."

If she answered or thanked me, I forget it. I was sensible of nothing at the moment but that the blood seemed flowing to my brain and thundering through it in ponderous waves. Then I knew we were walking down the passage, and in a few minutes more we should have said good-bye, and she would be gone. An acute and yet vague realisation came upon me that the corridor was dark, and the others had gone on in front, a confused recollection of the way she had lauded Nature and her domination a short time back, and then all these were lost again in the eddying torrent of an overwhelming desire to take her in my

86

arms and hold her, control her, assert my will over hers, this exasperating object who had been pleasing and seducing every sense for the last three hours, and now was leaving them all unsatisfied. That impulse towards some physical demonstration, that craving for physical contact which attacks us suddenly with its terrific impetus and chokes and stifles us ourselves beneath it, blinding us to all except itself, rushed upon me then walking beside her in the dark passage, and at that instant Theodora sighed.

"I am tired," she said languidly. "May I take your arm?" and her hand touched me.

I did not offer her my arm. I threw it round her neck, bending back her head upon it, so that her lips were just beneath my own as I leaned over her and I pressed mine on them in a delirium of passion. Everything that should have been remembered I forgot. Knowledge was lost of all except those passive burning lips under my own. As I touched them a current of madness seemed to mingle with my blood and pass flaming through all my veins. I heard her moan, but for that instant I was beyond the reach of pity or reason; I only leaned harder on her lips in a wild, unheeding, unsparing frenzy. It was a moment of ecstasy that I would have bought with years of my life. One moment, the next I released her, and so suddenly that she reeled against the wall of the passage. I caught her wrist to steady her. We dared neither of us speak, for the others were very little ahead of us, but I sought her eyes in the dusk. They met mine and rested on them, gleaming through the darkness; there was no confusion nor embarrassment in them; they were full of the hot, clear, blinding light of passion, and I knew there would be no need to crave forgiveness. The next moment had brought us up to the others, and to the end of the passage. Mrs. Strong turned round and held out her hand to me.

"Good-bye," she said. "We have had a most interesting afternoon."

It was with an effort that I made some conventional remark. Theodora, with perfect

A Man's Life

outward calm, shook hands with myself and
Digby with her sweetest smile, and passed out.

I lingered some few minutes with Digby
talking, and then he went off to his own
diggings, and I returned slowly down the
passage to my rooms. My blood and pulses
seemed beating as they do in fever, my ears
seemed full of sounds, and that kiss burned like
the brand of hot iron upon my lips.

When I reached my rooms I locked the door
and flung both the windows open to the snowy
night; the white powder on the ledge crumbled
and drifted in; an icy blast tore into the room
and made the blue and yellow flames of the
gas fire leap like demons over and amongst the
brick balls in the grate. I watched them for
a moment and then looked out: the brilliance
of the wintry night seemed to smite me. I
glanced up at the steady chill light of the stars.
Wide as the difference between their cold
gleams and the sinister small gas flames licking
the bars of my grate was the difference between
the passion a human being should inspire and
the passion I felt now. The old, eternal prob-

lem faced me, so well embodied in the three lines—

"Vis te Sexte coli volebam amare,
Parendum est tibi quod jubes colere,
Sed si te colo, Sexte non amabo."

They passed through and through my brain as I walked to and fro. I knew their truth, and, worse still, the truth of their converse— that where I loved I could not worship. Oh, to get rid of this fever in the blood, this torture of sense. To be able to think clearly without the vision of a human face swaying continually in one's brain, to shake off the close, clinging, serpent-like embrace of desire and stand free; free as a man is when no pulse, no thought resents control; when the brain in its cool, quiet order works like some perfect machine, of which each wheel and spring fulfils steadily its appointed function. And now all was broken, wrenched asunder, thrown into confusion, shattered; and what was left in place of that smooth-working mechanism? But the distorted, useless gear: disjointed thoughts, half-formed ideas, broken threads of plans, and

A Man's Life

whirling through them the torturing light of
two pale gleaming eyes. The humiliation and
agony of Lucretius, feeling the maddening
poison rioting through his blood, is that of
every man at some time in his life.

I sat by the fire with my head buried in my
hands. My desire claimed me for its own. I
could think of nothing but it. It forced me to
try and discover some means by which it might
be gratified or killed. That which I had done
forced further action upon me. A kiss in some
ranks means nothing, involves nothing, brings
no responsibility, but it is not so in ours.
Theodora would expect—and a cynical smile
crossed my face as I thought of it—a few lines
of passionate pleading to her to join her life
with mine. A tremendous temptation came
over me to send them. One wild, blind impulse
rose in me to take the present good and leave
all else to chance. I had nothing to lose,
nothing to suffer, and it was perhaps this that
helped me to stifle the continual, eager voice
within me, urging " Yield, yield."

If I had had any penalty to pay, it might

have blinded my eyes. I might have thought that I alone should have to pay the price; and therefore if I were willing to buy my happiness at that rate, I was free to do so; but here I saw that all the burden and all the sacrifice must fall on the loved one and not on me. My position would remain exactly the same whether I married Theodora or not. The money I should draw would be enough to support us both, and my plans need not be changed. My worldly ambition would not suffer. The presence of Theodora in my life would add a pleasure, an interest, a zest, a stimulus, and take nothing from it. I hardly dared to think of myself, nor of what our life would hold in it for me.

It was Theodora herself who must give up everything, and I nothing. I was prepared, in any case, for a life of poverty, discomfort, uncertainty, possibly danger. I left nothing behind me, and I went to seek something in the way of name or fame that I might or might not find; but she—she had everything life can offer at present. Could I ask her to blindly lay it

A Man's Life

all down and accept, without fore knowledge of
it, a life that had none of this world's goods in
it, and in which the only alleviation of its bar-
renness, the only consolation for its privations,
would be a man's passion?—a thing of which
she had no knowledge, no experience, and
which she might learn to loathe. And the step
would be irrevocable. With her marriage she
would become dependent: her life, now so
brilliant and secure, would be linked indis-
solubly with my hazardous, tumultuous, uncertain existence. It would be for her as if
she embarked from some safe and sunny port
in a slight, unseaworthy vessel on the changing,
varying sea; and the port would vanish—she
could never return to it. Henceforth she must
cling to the vessel or be left shelterless on the
strand; and if the vessel foundered, there would
remain but the bleak strand and the bleaker sea.

No, I could not: I could not ask, speak to
her. My lips were locked, and as the knowledge of my helplessness grew clearer, my duty
more sharply defined, the passion leaped higher
in my veins.

I hardly loved Theodora then. I think, with Balzac, that love for a woman comes after possession. Before, we are hardly conscious of anything but desire. Still, there had always been a struggling instinct in me, in all my passions, reprehensible though they might have been, to screen the objects of them, even from those very passions where they injured. It was this instinct now, when reason was eclipsed, that made me stumble mechanically over to my writing-table and draw a sheet of note-paper before me. But then I could not write. A delicate face traced itself before my eyes on the white expanse, with a male fire in the eyes, and a male curve of the determined lip, but the delicacy half froze my heart. Suppose it were ever my fate to see that face pale and fade from me into the shades of death, and know that I was responsible?

I took up my pen and wrote. I could not tell her the truth. I could not say it was for her own safety that I was writing as I was. If I did, I knew what she would answer. I was convinced that she would not have suffered,

A Man's Life

unresisting, such a kiss as mine had been unless she loved me, and love in a nature like Theodora's would lull to sleep reason, and sense, and self-command, and thought of self, and deliver her to me passive and chained.

I forced my unwilling hand to write a note in which I told her nothing. I merely apologised for what I had done. I was writing practically the death-warrant of my own wishes, for an apology under the circumstances would mean a disclaimer of my love, and every irritated, excited fibre in my system revolted violently from each word I wrote. However, I got through it at last, and rose from the table with every nerve on edge, and feeling as if the walls of the room were approaching on all sides to crush me in the narrow space. Was it necessary? was it absolutely clear that I ought to deny her to myself when I knew she loved me, or was it merely a Quixotism to be laughed at? If I could believe that it were! But, no, it seemed to me perfectly monstrous to take her from her present state and make her my wife, though she consented a thousand

times over. Her consent valued nothing,
since she had no knowledge of myself and
no realisation of that which sharing my life
would mean. These must come after she had
made an irrevocable sacrifice, after she had
left herself helpless and dependent upon me.
Her consent, her will, her strenuous wish even
had nothing to do with the question. They
were like a man's signature to a document he
has not read. I must decide for her, I who
knew the document by heart. It was not her
mere income that was of worth to her, it was
her peculiarly independent and uncontrolled
position, the habit of command and influence,
that she must give up with it. And still, even
all these considerations I might have been
tempted to set aside had I held a higher
opinion of myself, had I thought I was a
thoroughly good fellow, with qualities calculated to repay a woman for any sacrifice. I
tried to recall the different opinions and
remarks and verdicts I had heard at various
times on myself and my conduct—all laughed
at, at the time, but now suddenly become of

A Man's Life

value. Could I have recalled a good one now it would have given the keenest pleasure. I remembered I had been called callous, egotistical, indifferent, cold, heartless, dissolute, conceited—all these men had said to me and of me. Clever! Yes—many, most people had called me that. This quality had been generally coupled with whichever opprobrious epithet others had thought justified in bestowing on me. Clever! The blood passed over my face as the recollection cut in upon me of what Theodora had said. Suddenly they recurred to me, her words and my own sneer. The quality she looked for in a man was intellect. Well, good. But that was but one point in a whole character in my favour.

Now for my life. I stared absently down on the ground, thinking, throwing my mental glance back through it to the beginning—that is to the beginning of man's life, in my case to the end of the fifteenth year. From then till now, this space of fourteen years, I looked at critically, and this was absolutely clear, that I, from my point of view, found nothing to condemn. But I was considering now from others' standpoint, not my own; and the few people who had known my life, or thought they had, had said it was evil, and insisted that my seeing nothing reprehensible in my actions was the worst point I had. This argument itself is one of which the cogency escapes me. To commend a man because he knows he is doing wrong while he is and continues doing it has always been impossible to me. It must prove the greatest depth of degradation or of weakness. When some such remark as the following has been made to me—" I say, do you think that's the right thing to do, what you're doing?" I have always said with surprise, " Most emphatically, or I should not do it," and it has not been a form, but the simplest, barest truth. However, I believe men hold that one who takes his pleasure, whatever it may be, and then when the temptation and error is past says in excuse, " I knew all the time I was acting like a brute, but I could not help it," stands on a higher rung in the ladder of virtue than a man

A Man's Life

like myself. He has more conscience. Also,
it has been said to me that my defence that
my pleasure has never made another's misery
has no weight and cannot count in the balance
of morality. If I consider it the main point,
that shows how degenerate I am.

No; those fourteen years would be full of
evil. My past life would be accounted bad from
the standpoint of others—perhaps from hers
then. And yet in a sudden, hot glow of
pleasure I thought not, as the vision of that
intellectual, all-comprehending, indulgent smile,
and the lips that had formed it, rushed up
through the gloom and dusk of my room before
my eyes. I thought—I thought—but I had no
business to think, to assume things in my favour.
Theodora might—I did not believe it from what
I had seen—but still she might wake after her
first dream of passion to be terrified at the
recklessness and the disregard of all accepted
rules of life in the man to whom she belonged.
I could not then free her and replace her in her
own life any more than she could free herself,
nor could I change my own nature. As for con-

cealment or deception, I was far too innately
indolent and too absolutely cynical to tolerate
it in any intimate relation. Then, in conclusion, my life, like my character, must be
accounted against me. What, then, remained
to offer her in exchange for everything she
now possessed? Nothing but a few good looks,
and even these half spoiled by dissipation and
bad habits. And supposing these were powerful,
even deteriorated as they were, it seemed im-
measurably mean, unspeakably contemptible to
trade upon them for my own desires. A look, a
glance can catch the senses and hold them, and
lull the reason to sleep for a time as nothing
else can do; and worst of all the reason does
not only sleep, but dreams that all else is in
harmony. Theodora's sensitive eye would extract some pleasure from my face, and then all
else would be supplied to me, whatever qualities
she wanted me to possess, by her imagination.
And to think of this revolted me. To let her see
the looks, and hence assume the character,
seemed to me despicable—allied to the trading
instinct of a merchant selling wares, as vile as

A Man's Life

the action of the dealer who puts fresh fruit on the top of his basket, knowing all beneath is rotten. God! it was monstrous! I could not do it. Better ten million times to forego her. Better far for me to take the pain and the suffering on myself now and alone than see her irrevocably yoked to it later.

I came up to the table again, picked up the letter with a decided hand, and went out. I took the letter to the end of the street and posted it. Then I went on to Digby's rooms, and sat up playing cards with him and drinking brandy all night. At five in the morning I was very drunk, and Digby saw me home. I noticed in a clouded way how those beastly flames were still playing round the bricks in the grate when I got up to my rooms. I had lost a lot of money, and was so intoxicated that I could only stagger to my bed and fling myself upon it, dressed as I was. No matter. The letter had gone. My decision was made, and Theodora was saved.

The next day I had so bad a headache that study was out of the question. I could hardly think. In the evening a letter came from her. I tore it open. It consisted of three lines :—

"Thank you for your letter. As to pardon, I have none to give, for in my eyes you have not erred."

That was all. The blood rushed burning over my face as I read. So that was not an error in her eyes. I laughed aloud in the silent, empty room—a dreary laugh at my own thoughts. Would anything be? Anything that I did? Perhaps not. But, after all, would that justify me in my own eyes—the simple fact that she might condone or forgive me for crimes against her? No. It was well that I had decided as I had. A kiss! Well, what was a kiss, after all? It might be a moral sin on the part of the giver—a moral shame on the part of the receiver—but there was no injury done, no suffering entailed. Let my transgressions against her cease there. I would not see her again, nor write to her, except a line of fare-well, before I left. I took the letter that had left her hand and kissed it till the ink grew blurred and faint under my lips; then I flung it into the flames.

102

CHAPTER IV.

THE few weeks that remained of my stay in London I used for seeing old friends before I left, getting a few things I needed, and idling generally. I saw and heard nothing of Theodora, and I tried hard to erase her image from the tablets of my mind. But as each day brought me nearer to the hour for starting, my depression grew upon me. I could not shake off the thought that I was going away from her voluntarily, perhaps never to see her again. The deserts and the solitudes, the excavations and the ruins, had lost all charm: I thought more of a dark eyebrow and the touch of a slight, burning hand. All pleasure in the expedition had gone. A tremendous reaction had followed the sudden storm of passion that Theodora had aroused, and though the storm had passed over, the deadly apathy towards all other objects, and towards life itself, that had succeeded, was—or might be if I yielded to it— as fatal to success. I struggled hard against it. I told myself a dozen times a day that it was but the reaction and must pass, and I went on with all my preparations in the teeth of it. Everything was mechanically done, and without any heart or spirit being put into it. Still it was done, and the day fixed on for leaving came and found me, at six o'clock in the evening, sitting in my chambers, my two portmanteaux packed, all my charts and maps stripped from the wall, the narrow room entirely dismantled. I was leaving by the evening Dover train from Victoria. I had begged my friends not to come and see me off. I did not wish to be made to feel I was taking a solemn and eternal farewell of England.

"My dear fellow," I had said to Digby, "I am so uncertain: I may be back again in a year's time, and off somewhere else, and then you'll have all this goodbye-ing to do over again. It's waste of time."

So now I sat alone. Everything was finished,

A Man's Life

and it was yet too early to start for the station. I fell to wondering in a vague way whether Theodora had cared much or little or not at all when she had heard that I was going. She had not answered my letter, but that told me nothing.

"There is a gentleman to see you, sir."

"That confounded Digby, after all," I thought.

"He can come in," I said to the boy, and turned to find the lucifers.

Before I had succeeded in this, however, I heard a quick step, a figure passed swiftly into the room and came up to me in the darkness, and the next moment there was the burning clasp of another hand upon mine. That touch! Could I ever fail to recognise it? I knew it was Theodora's hand. That hand of velvet, with all its tiny bones so flexible and so easily crushable, and yet with such a tremendous fire in the smooth palm. And the sudden touch of it seemed to send a river of pain through my whole body—or was it pleasure? It is hard to say: these two in their intensity are almost one. Then through the darkness came a voice, her voice, but strained, thin, and sharp with agonised shame and fear—·

"Cecil! you are not angry with me?"

"Angry, Theodora! How could I be angry with you?" I answered.

I was standing still. My heart seemed to have ceased beating, the blood to be held checked in my veins. My only thought was that she had come to say good-bye to me, and between the excitement her presence always roused in me and the terror that it might lead me to undo what I had done for her sake, I was held immovable and almost speechless.

"Why have you come, dear?" I murmured, hardly audible.

She gave a strained, hysterical laugh.

"You are all in the dark," she said. "Now!" and she suddenly struck a match of her own and put it to the gas burner over our heads.

"Now, does my dress tell you nothing?"

The gas blazed up, and she stood under the full flare of it, and I saw then that she was dressed in an ordinary suit of man's clothes and a fur-lined overcoat. I saw these things indeed, but my gaze was fixed upon her face and the nervous, widely-dilated eyes, that, full of an agony of confusion as they were, yet met and remained on mine. A hot line of carmine glowed feverishly beneath them on the otherwise blanched face. The fear, pain, and terrible excitement on the delicate countenance went to my heart and pierced it through its own tumultuous, expectant delight.

"Explain," I said very gently, and I closed my right hand firmly over hers. "Theodora, you know you may say anything freely to me."

"You are going to-night," she said, giving a fleeting glance round the room, and then bringing her burning eyes back to my face, "and I have come to go with you, if you wish. Cecil, I know you care for me," and I saw her lips whiten from the excitement that forced the words from her. "I am convinced of it. Otherwise, of course . . . of course . . . And some idea, some myth, is separating us. You said you wanted to take some friend, some companion with you, only you knew no one you cared for sufficiently. Then you said it would be impossible to take a wife there, don't you remember? That the life wouldn't suit a woman, or something. But you did say you wished there was some nice fellow who could go out with you. Well, let me come, Cecil, instead!" She trembled excessively; the hand in mine fluttered convulsively; her face paled till even the flush of shame died out of it. "I have taken this dress so as to be no trouble to you. No one will know who I am, nor guess that I am a woman. Now, would they ever?"

And she stepped a little back from me and raised her face towards the light. And I looked at her, and my brain seemed suddenly to reel. Here was what I had been desiring and craving put into my very hands freely, without cost to me, without the least sacrifice demanded in return. This form I coveted was here, instinct with life, and the double life lent it at this moment by its passions. This torturer of my dreams, this disturber of my waking moments was here, clothed in the actual, tangible, visible, desirable beauty of the flesh, demanding nothing but that I should take and enjoy it, within reach of my hand, and nothing between us except unwritten laws. The great unwritten laws of Self and the Other, and these seemed like some huge hand that kept me from her.

I turned from her sharply and took a few steps towards the window, and fixed my eyes on the blank panes, anywhere, so that they were not on that nervous, trembling, excited frame. For a second it seemed I could not summon enough self-control to speak to her. For a second my command seemed fallen amongst the clamour of the senses, as the driver's reins under the trampling hoofs of his team. There was a second or two of silence, and then, with my hand on the throat of my own desire, I walked back to her where she stood on my hearth.

"Theodora, you don't realise the sacrifice you are making, but I do, and it is too great. I cannot accept it. It is impossible."

Theodora paled till she was whiter than the ash in the grate.

"Sacrifice! Cecil, what do you mean? I am making no sacrifice. I am simply striving after my own great wish."

Six Chapters of

The unsparing knowledge of self, and the open confession to it that lay in the liquid eyes meeting mine, took the place of another woman's confusion. It was not so difficult to speak to her as it would have been to a more childish intelligence. I did not dare to touch her, nor take her hand. It was as much as I could do to look at her and still speak.

"It may be your own wish now," I said. "But unconsciously you are paying too high a price for it. Think what your life is. You have everything in it that money can give. You may not value it because you have it, and have always had it; but you would regret it. You will give up everything, and I have nothing to give you to replace it—absolutely nothing."

"Except yourself; except your looks, and the fact that you are the man I—— Oh, you don't understand!" she added vehemently. "It is worth all those things!"

"Yes, I do understand," I said, feeling myself pale and colour momentarily with the stress of those impulses she was either purposely or unconsciously exciting. "I understand much

110

A Man's Life

better than you do. The first fortnight I should
be able to compensate you for everything, and
after that—what then? A bare hut on a stretch
of sand, a fearful climate, no possible occupation
or distraction, no human being but myself to
speak to, no society but that of a herd of native
workmen, every kind of hardship, and above all
the probable sickness and disease to suffer,—
this for you, coming from your life of pleasure
and independence, surrounded by amusement,
flattery, and every sort of gratification; where
you have only to form a wish to have it fulfilled!
I couldn't let you make the change, Theodora.
You would inevitably regret it, and then I
should have no power to give these things back
to you. However you repented afterwards,
neither of us could undo the step; you could
never get back the position you have now. I
shall be a poor man all my life; and, dearest,
passion is a thing of months at best; life is a
thing of years, or may be."

Theodora turned and stretched out her arms
upon the mantelpiece, and laid her head down
upon them.

"Equally, life is not measured by years but by enjoyment," she answered in a low tone. "There is nothing you can say, Cecil, which I have not thought of. I have weighed and considered all these things, and my own mind is absolutely made up. The future to the future. We are both living in this hour, and that is all we can call our own." There was a desperate, strained silence between us. My dizzy brain was striving to collect the nervous, feverish thoughts and disentangle them for speech, and then suddenly Theodora threw back her head and looked at me. Her eyes were blazing with appealing, supplicating desire, her face changed from white to a flame of scarlet and then back again to almost grey. She stood close to me, as close as it is possible to be without actual contact, so close that the warmth of her being fell distinctly upon mine.

"Cecil, it is not in me to care for any man who is indifferent to me. This passion was born in your own kiss. It was then and not till then, only then, that I made a vow—within two weeks I am this man's. But if now, honestly, in honour, you can look into my eyes and say you do not love me as I thought, I will leave you this minute."

Her gaze searched my face keenly. This was what I had always thought, that Theodora's love was but the result of mine; that from the first she had loved my passion for herself, clothed in a form that had happened to catch her fancy and please her senses. Those natures that are intensely responsive, as hers, are the last to give spontaneously. The tendency to eagerly and readily respond is often confused with the tendency to offer unasked, but in reality these two are exactly opposite. This extreme sensitiveness to emotion in another, this sympathetic excitability proves the absence rather than the presence of an ability to fall into any particular state of feeling without exterior excitement. I felt if I had not lost my self-command, if I had not, as I had, virtually told her, though with closed lips, that I loved her, she would never have sought me, nor ever felt a pulse beat quicker at the thought of me. And now the opportunity was here to undo the evil I had done, or at least to prevent the greater resultant evil of accepting her complete sacrifice. If I chose to act the part well, if I told her she had been misled, if I hinted I was unwilling or indifferent, I knew I could drive her from me without difficulty—and drive her from me not to despair, nor even great or long regret, as might be the case with a differently constituted woman, but simply back to her former life. Once convince her that I had no desire for her, her own would die, wither. I knew it without her telling me. Her extreme susceptibility, mental and physical, denied the power to love without return. There would be no tears, no despairing draught of poison. I could imagine her going back with a reckless openness and indifference to her disguise, and facing her sister with a careless laugh. And as for me, one slight sentence would be sufficient: "Oh yes, he had got over his fancy for me! I offered to go with him, but—" and here a laugh and a shrug of her shoulders. "I never saw a fellow so frigid!" It all passed in a painful flash

A Man's Life

through me, and the idea that I ought perhaps
in this way to force her back into security, but
it passed from me as quickly as it came. Not
even for her sake would I look into her eyes
and swear a lie. And nothing short of this
would be of any avail. To tell her that myself
was as unworthy of her as my worldly position,
to speak of my vices and the character I possessed amongst my friends, to prove the small
likelihood of my rendering her life a happy one,
I saw would all be useless. To tell a woman,
blinded by physical desire, of the imperfections
of her lover, is like throwing straws against a
brick wall. Nothing would save her now except a deliberate, lying denial of my own
passion, and this I was too naturally honourable or too naturally selfish to be able to force
to my lips.

"Well, Cecil," she said, and her voice had
an infinite seduction in it, the whole inflection
of reason overthrown, "can you say you do
not want me?" And she raised one arm and
put her hand round my neck above the collar.

There was just a tinge of mockery on the

soft dividing lips, a shade of provoking scorn on the whole charming face raised to me, that stung me as she meant it should; but even in that instant, above the fierce desires struggling for uncontrolled sway within me, rose that knowledge of danger for her that had protected her from me up till now.

As a man in nightmare or delirium tries with his slight, feeble arms to ward off the host of huge, horrible, overpowering, indefinable presences that crowd in upon his bed, so I instinctively put forth as a shield before the destructive blaze of our own passions the next thin, frail, useless, foolish words.

"Would it not be better to wait for me till I return? When I may have more to offer, and when at least I need not take you into danger?"

"Wait! perhaps I might have said 'Yes' at fifteen, but I am three-and-twenty, and I have not yet known happiness and love. Fate has always withheld her two greatest gifts. Cecil, are you going to withhold them too?"

With that last appeal she swept from me

A Man's Life

the remnant of my power to check the impulses within me. Her last words had a
bitter reproach in them, and they stung me
beyond endurance. I felt the tremendous flood
of rebellious eager passion she had roused
surging through me, the all-conquering, all-
destroying tide in which our highest and our
lowest feelings mix and mingle. One great
impulse, one instinct urged and spurred me—
to confer that happiness, if indeed I could,
which she said she coveted and I denied. I
crushed the soft, hot hand within my own,
and threw my other arm round her shoulders,
drawing her close to my breast, pressing her
to it, and kissed her. There was no need of
words. In my touch, in my eyes, in the beat
of the pulse in the arm round her neck, she
must have read all and been satisfied. Theodora suffered it, but she did not respond,
actively. She gave me no kiss nor the faintest
caress in return. She merely sank, yielded to
my embrace, lay in it as her hand had lain
in mine. Some women inflame us by their
resistance, others by their compliance. It

was this last with Theodora. It was her sudden, complete abandonment of self, the entire throwing away of her own will, the apparent absolute merging of all volition into another's, that must have always set ablaze all the manhood of a man who loved her. Like a soft snake within one's grasp, like a thick parasite creeper lying along a branch, she had sunk into my arms and her head was heavy upon my shoulder. She seemed in those moments will-less, soulless, mentally and physically powerless, the mere incarnation of devotion to another, of absolute submission.

There are infinite variations in the manner of receiving an embrace corresponding to the infinite varieties of women, from the laughing resistance of the pretty *débutante* to the serious passion of a woman whose violent response forms one-half of it; from the innocent, childlike return given by the mindless schoolgirl, to the chaste restraint of the woman who withdraws chillingly after the first kiss. But no woman has ever met my arms as

A Man's Life

Theodora did, with such a strange, almost terrible surrender of personal will. And no woman has ever moved me one millionth part as much. This intense, burning, silent passivity, this very unresponsiveness of the nervous frame, seemed to constitute a tremendous, infinite demand; to be the expression of a boundless longing to be loved; a desire that would absorb all that one could give and yet would be unsatisfied; and the intensity, the illimitability of the demand roused my passion and my will to meet it to their utmost height. As no other woman has ever done, she seemed to give a tremendous challenge to my desire for herself, my vanity, and mere nature, and all three leaped up in an uncalculated, unmeasured, mad response. Was it a second or a minute, a minute or half-an-hour, that I held her? I could not tell. Time is not measured, as she had said, by number, but by sensation. The next thing in my memory was her voice saying, "Then you will take me with you?" And I answered, "Yes, I will take you."

Six Chapters of

"Let us go now before we are prevented. We have no time to lose."

With an effort I released her and turned my eyes away from her. They fell on the ready strapped portmanteaux. Luggage, cabs, railways, catching and losing trains, these were the things I tried to bend my delirious thoughts to and calm them by recalling what had to be done. I drew out my watch mechanically.

"We might still catch that train," I said, feeling in an unreal dream. Was Theodora, after all, coming with me? Was it "we" and not "I" any longer? "You have no things, of course?"

"None. But I brought money with me. I shall be no expense to you."

"That's unworthy of you!" I said, with a flush of pain at her words. "You know——"

"Yes, I know," said Theodora impulsively. "You would give me all you had, but then I feel just the same, and so I brought all I could." And she drew out a pocket-book with, apparently, notes in it.

A Man's Life

"Keep it then," I said, turning her hand aside, and rang for the boy to take my luggage.

While we stood waiting I looked at her critically for the first time. The disguise was perfect, as she said. Both face and figure yielded completely to the character given them by the dress. The tremendous mass of hair had been cut away, and what was left curled now close round the head in resentful curls, and it would have been difficult for any one to believe that the pale, brilliant face with its straight features and dark line on the upper lip, was not that of some handsome boy of nineteen or twenty.

We went down to the door, and had the portmanteaux put on a hansom and drove to Victoria. In the cab I asked her how she had made up her mind to sacrifice that lovely hair. Theodora gave a laugh that sounded above the clatter of the hansom, and I felt her hand seek mine, upon my knee, and close on it.

"My dear Cecil!" she said, turning to me with her eyebrows raised, "I would have paid with my life for these hours with you! Do you suppose I care a hang about my hair? It was such a great bunch," she went on, laughing, "to cut off, and then I didn't know in the least what to do with it. It nearly put the fire out, and wodged up all the grate. However, I burned it up at last."

I was silent. The light, careless words in the mocking voice conveyed an indefinite reproach to my ears. It might be a slight thing in itself, this first sacrifice, but it seemed to me the sinister beginning of an evil series. Her very recklessness of self, in tone and thought stirred a strange, nameless sensation of mingled delight and dread. It threw a heavier responsibility still upon me. It left a delicious, limitless power in my hands, and I saw she would be too heedless, too careless, too confident in me, to think of restraining me if I used it ill. The next moment, on the flood of personal pleasure that filled me, the pitying, compassionate thoughts drifted from my mind like whirling straws in a torrent.

When we got into the station, the Dover

A Man's Life

train was drawn up, ready to leave the platform. There was only just time to have my luggage thrown into the van and get our tickets.

"We must get a carriage alone," I said, as we hurried down the train. "Here's this—First Smoking. This will do."

We got in and took our seats at the end of the empty carriage. I had drawn the rug over Theodora and the blind across the window to shut out the icy draught, and the train was already in motion when the door was torn open and another passenger plunged in upon us. His bag followed, and the door was slammed to behind him. We both scanned him hastily, but it was no one we knew: only an ordinary stranger who had intruded upon us at the last minute.

"Confound him," I murmured, and Theodora looked at me and laughed.

The night was arctic. The steam froze rapidly into an opaque sheet over the window. The air in the carriage was so cold that it brought a numbing, soporific influence with it.

We all three smoked hard to keep up some
attempt at warmth, and I drew up Theodora's
fur collar round her neck and asked her if she
felt the cold very much. As she looked up
with her quick smile, I saw the marks of
fatigue and sleeplessness like livid bruises under
her eyes.

"You are tired. Put your head down on
my shoulder and go to sleep," I said, putting
my arm round her waist.

"Won't that look too affectionate?" she
murmured back with a glance at our companion in the corner. "We must be careful."

"Hang him," I answered. "Never mind
what it looks; it doesn't matter."

Theodora laid her head down on my shoulder
with a contented sigh, and her lids fell heavily
over her eyes. The fellow in the corner peered
curiously at us round his *Globe*, and looked
intently at the white face on my arm. I
opened my own paper and held it up in my
right hand before us to shade the light from
her eyes, and my own face from criticism, as I
looked down at her.

A Man's Life

When we were only a short distance from Dover I spoke to her. She looked up immediately. Our companion had fallen asleep in his corner.

"You are tired, Theodora, too tired to cross to-night. Let us stop in Dover and go on to-morrow morning," I said.

The colour leaped over her face, and she answered quickly, "Oh no, Cecil! Let us go on. You would if you were alone, wouldn't you?"

"Yes, I was going straight through to Marseilles; but, darling, there is no hurry. You are very tired—let us stay here to-night," and I pressed her tightly to me.

"No, Cecil, I don't want to," she said decidedly, and then, with a flash from under the white lids, "You know you are not thinking of my being tired!"

I coloured and loosened my arm.

"And is it a great crime?" I murmured, looking at her.

"Well, but any way, don't ask me to stay—please don't; let's go straight on."

She looked so excited and distressed that I could do nothing but yield.

"Certainly. Of course, it shall be as you like," I answered.

It was an excessively cold night for crossing. Theodora and I were both too restless to go below. We walked up and down the deck, talking for the most part in rather a strained way on indifferent subjects, of which we were neither of us thinking—at least I was not. My mind would keep reverting to the inexplicable way women have of treating, one may say, their own wishes.

A man will always take the quickest, shortest route to the fulfilment of his desires, and seize his enjoyment the moment he can get it. But a woman, with her desire within reach, will hold aloof from it till the last possible moment, even at the imminent risk of losing it altogether.

Theodora's passion must have been equal to my own, considering she had thrown over every material and personal advantage merely to gratify it, and yet, not even for the gravest and weightiest reasons would I have deferred

our pleasure now, as she did, for no reason
whatever. I could not pay attention to what
she was saying. I was wondering how, with
all that fever burning in the soft, tremulous
arm and hand resting on mine, she could
persist in prolonging these strained, uneasy
relations, and in torturing me with this formal,
decorous talk about the stars and what not.

When we reached Paris, between six and
seven the following morning, I urged the same
thing again—that we might pause here—with
the same result, a rigid refusal, and when I
pressed the point, a burst of excited tears.

"Leave me in peace till Marseilles, Cecil,"
she reiterated, her face burning and turning
her eyes away from me, as we sat over our
coffee in the Paris waiting-room.

I shall never forget how irresistibly charming
she looked at that moment to my eyes, as
she sat opposite me on the horse-hair railway
couch, the fur over-coat thrown open at her
white neck, and the small dark head and
straight features outlined against the grimy
waiting-room wall as she turned from me with

flushed cheeks and tremulous lips, and brimming eyes.

"But why?" I persisted. "At Marseilles, perhaps, you will say the same thing. We can't go on travelling perpetually; we may as well stay here as anywhere."

"But I don't want to. Why, you've admitted you were going on to Marseilles without stopping if you had been alone."

"It is nonsense to talk of what I should have done if I had been alone!" I said, flushing. "To have you with me like this, and to be alone, are two totally different things!"

I could not trust myself to speak further. I got up and left her there, feeling a gust of irritated anger eclipse my love for her.

Love! It is a pity to so debase the word.

I went on to the platform and walked up and down it.

I have a strong leaning to the qualities and attributes of my own sex, and now Theodora was acting in the most feminine way, and displaying that most aggravating trait in women, of seeming inability to come to the point in

A Man's Life

anything. Moreover, I had a keen suspicion
that another feminine and very contemptible
motive was at work—the delight that women
take in testing a man, and seeing how much he
can endure without losing his head. However,
after a few turns, I took a gentler view.

Was it not natural that a girl like this,
taught from her first years to regard modesty
and chastity as next to or dearer than her life
itself, as an inseparable, integral part of every
phrase or action, should feel an almost insuper-
able, involuntary shrinking before the first
violent uprooting of these ingrained, ingrown
habits? Not even the impetus of passion can
wholly sweep away the clinging impressions of
three-and-twenty years. It was these, rather
than anything else, that were against me. And
could I wish these absent? No; it was clear
that I was a brute. And, full of humiliation,
I hurried back to her. She had not moved.

" Forgive me for speaking as I did," I said
gently. " We will go on to Marseilles by the
9 A.M. train. But promise me that you won't
insist farther."

She looked up, with the colour flooding all her face.

"I promise, Cecil. I've said it."

We made no further allusion to the matter, and took the nine train southwards from the Lyons station.

Theodora recovered all her natural gaiety and ease with me. She made no objection to my choosing a carriage empty save for ourselves, and paying the guard to keep it so. She did insist, however, on our maintaining opposite sides of the carriage.

"Take that nice, comfortable corner," she said, laughing, and throwing herself into the other directly opposite. "I have lots to talk to you about, and I find that you pay practically no attention whatever when you are beside me!"

I obeyed and sat down opposite her. She got out of her pocket a packet of cigarette papers and began to roll up cigarettes.

"Don't you want to know how I got away and came to you?" she said after a minute.

"Very much; but, after all, the great point is that you did it."

A Man's Life

" First tell me, Cecil, do you like my dress, and me in it ? "

She flushed and spoke with visible hesitation. I had not liked to allude to her dress, nor notice it more than I could help, for fear of embarrassing her. Now that she asked me, I cast my eyes over her figure with undisguised admiration.

" You look adorable in it; and the turn-out is first-rate. How did you get it ? "

" I went to a tailor's in Bond Street and told them I was going to a fancy dress ball as a nineteenth century masher," she said, offering me the cigarettes she had been making, " and that I wanted a perfect fit out, the best they could do, and that I did not care what the bill came to as long as I was satisfied. I said I wanted afternoon clothes, not evening. The fur overcoat I bought there too, saying I should want it after the ball. The clothes were sent up to the house, but my own maid took them in, as I had ordered her to, and she might have thought they were tailor-made dresses. Well then, when I tried them on and looked in the glass, and knew I was coming to you in them, I laughed. I thought I looked very nice in them; they happen to suit my face and figure and all that; but, you know, it seemed very funny. Girls are always represented as trying on their wedding dress and orange blossoms, and thinking their lover will admire them in it. But, somehow, as I looked at my own reflection, I felt certain that you would not mind this in place of the orthodox white satin!"

I was silent for a few seconds, then I said, looking her full in the face, "You were quite right in divining that I should not mind you in this dress, and that I am not a stickler for orthodoxy and white satin; but still, I should have preferred to marry you, and I shall insist on doing so at the first opportunity."

Theodora raised her eyebrows and burst out laughing. "What a tone, Cecil! Why, I have no objection to marriage! On the contrary, I think it is an excellent institution; but in our particular case we had to dispense with it, and in our case it does not matter. Of course, your housemaid must marry her young man with

A Man's Life

whom she walks out on Sunday or she comes
to grief, we all know. But I have no fear of
your cruel desertion of me, nor that I shall
have to play the part of seducee!"

"No, no, my dearest, I know. But you must
see that I can't bear that you should put yourself in a false position, even for a time, for my
sake."

Theodora shrugged her shoulders.

"Well, I could hardly come to your rooms in
the orange flower turn-out and say, ' Marry me.'
And you wouldn't ask me, and so—and so—
hence the tears, if there are any; but I don't
see that it matters a straw. It is you who are
fussing."

I leaned forward and seized her two dear
little hands.

"You must know why I did not ask you.
You must know it was because I thought I had
no right—considering all you had to give up,
and that I had nothing to offer—no right to
make you my wife."

"As it is, I shall be your mistress, and that
will be worse!" retorted Theodora, with a lovely

and tormenting smile. "I warned you not to attempt the impossible. Mortal things are fitting to mortals. How could you hope to wall up our love by your little orthodoxies, and considerations, and fears? You excited a tremendous—well, what shall I say to sound well?—a tremendous emotion in me. You saw that you had done it, and then you suddenly take it into your head that it will be inestimably for my benefit for you to go away without satisfying it! You are a funny mixture!"

I buried my head in my hands.

"Yes, I know. I am an execrable wretch!"

She stroked my hair backwards and forwards.

"It is all very nice and satisfactory and convenient as it is," she said, laughing, "and you have nothing on earth to worry about. When we go back I'll turn out in regular British matron style, and you shall marry me two or three times over to make up, if you like."

It was impossible not to laugh with her.

"As to what I have given up, you know the line referring to tents and thrones. I have

A Man's Life

tried the thrones, so to speak, and not liked them——"

"You may not like the tents any better," I interrupted, jesting too, but with a certain seriousness I could not shake off.

"The tents! no, I have no predilection for an empty tent, but if it is the dwelling-place of Cecil Ray- ——"

Her eyes finished the sentence for her.

"Now, Theodora, if you are going to talk like that, you can't expect me to remain on this side of the carriage!"

"Well, I'm not going to talk like it, then. No, really; stay where you are. We are not anywhere near Marseilles yet!"

Silence.

Then she said, a shade coming over her face, "The only thing I am sorry about is leaving Hester. It was a tremendous wrench. I left a letter for her explaining everything, so she will feel no anxiety about me, and I suppose she will invent some graceful lie for outsiders."

Another pause, which she broke by asking, "How long are we going to stop at Marseilles?"

"About a week, I suppose," I answered. "To enable you to get some things, and so on."

Theodora nodded.

"And then where do we go?"

"Aden. There is no need, you see, for me to hurry. I thought we might go through the Red Sea and Persian Gulf and drop down upon Baghdad that way."

"Very good," returned Theodora, piling up two French novels for a pillow, and then stretching herself full-length on her own side of the carriage without the least embarrassment, looking desperately captivating and graceful as she did so.

" By the way——"

" Well?"

"You won't forget and call me Theodora by mistake before people, will you? It is quite easy to drop the *a* and put an *e* instead. When I was christened, I suppose my parents noticed I was very like a boy, and so with admirable forethought gave me a name that would do for either!"

" No, I shall not forget."

A Man's Life

She looked at me and exclaimed suddenly,
"Cecil, you look dreadfully pale! what is the
matter?"

"Do I? Nothing, dearest! What should
there be?"

"What are you thinking of?"

"Of how confoundedly wide these carriages
are for one thing!"

Theodora laughed and changed the subject.

At Lyons, as we slowed down, she suggested
that I should get out.

"Go to the bar and get a brandy-and-soda—
at any rate, the fresh air on the platform. Do."

"Will you come?"

"No; that's no use. You go; I'll wait for
you."

I laughed and declined, and remained where
I was. In those moments I was as absolutely
chained and helpless, bound by every indomi-
table instinct to remain in her presence and
proximity, even though denied contact with her,
as if a thousand rivets and bars were holding
me on either side.

We paused at Lyons only about ten minutes,

and then the train swung on through the darkness.

At last, towards midnight, we came into Marseilles. Theodora, who had been talking and laughing, with an excited gaiety literally overflowing her sparkling eyes, abruptly became silent as we stopped. Our eyes met involuntarily, and she seemed to shrink before the glance of triumph I threw over her. We neither of us spoke. I got out and handed her to the platform. It so happened that the omnibus to take us to the hotel filled up rapidly as our fellow-passengers, all men, crowded into it. There was room for ten inside, and as Theodora and I were taking our places an eleventh passenger hurried up. He was a corpulent Frenchman, who lamented loudly there was no place for him. I turned to him instantly and begged him to come in: there was quite room for him, as I and my friend would take only one seat. Then I looked at Theodora, who had not yet taken her place. She was helpless, as the omnibus was too low-roofed to permit any one to stand, and I took her into

A Man's Life

my longing arms and drew her down on my
knees. The fat Frenchman, profuse in thanks,
hurried in; the door slammed, and the omnibus
started. We were almost in darkness. A lamp
at the farther end of the vehicle sent down only
a jolted flicker at intervals. The Frenchmen
gabbled together incessantly. Theodora and I
did not utter one word. I was simply submerged in my own feelings, and incapable of
speech; and she—I don't know what passed in
her brain, but her breath seemed stifled and
suffocated as she drew it. I felt her heart
beating frantically, like a trapped bird's, as I
pressed her against my breast, and the slight
waist heaved convulsively under my arm. Once
the wheel of the omnibus was caught, and it
swayed violently. The word "Collision" went
from mouth to mouth, and I felt myself turn
pale. An accident to-night! The thought
could turn me into a coward; to-morrow, if
the world split into its billion atoms, I felt I
should not care, had I once finally and utterly
made her my own.

We did reach the hotel at last, while I was

questioning madly whether we ever should, and went with the other passengers to the coffee-room. I had never seen Theodora look lovelier from a purely physical point of view than she did as we took our seats at the table—more appealing and more seductive. The mental, intellectual charm was less perhaps, or possibly I myself was unable just then, in the tumultuous pleasure of the senses, to be conscious of it. The heat of the room, after the outside cold, had warmed the blood; the brightest scarlet ran through the smooth, smiling lips and glowed faintly beneath the pale skin of the cheeks; the long Egyptian-cut eyes were wide and dark and nervously expanded, scintillating like two mirrors beneath which a lamp is held; and the gaslight, coming down in a flood upon her head, tinged the short, loose waves of black hair with gold. I saw the waiter eyeing her with great interest from time to time as he laid our table, and at last he could restrain his gossiping, curious nature no longer, and said inquiringly, "Monsieur, c'est un Italien comme moi?" It was thundering cheek on his part, and I felt

A Man's Life

inclined to get up and leave the table; but the falseness of our position and the effeminate look that the painted eyes lent the face opposite me checked me, and Theodora herself laughed and answered the man in his own tongue. I don't know Italian, so I could not follow what she said to him, but I supposed it was some chaff, for she sent him away highly delighted and shaking with laughter. A minute after he was back again with a tray of his best cigars and cigarettes and his most finely polished glasses. When he had disappeared I said:

"You had better discontinue putting that stuff on your eyes. It did not matter when you were in your own character, but it excites notice now."

I was half afraid she would be offended, as nine out of ten other women would have been at a similar speech, and that was why I had not spoken about it before. But Theodora only gave her usual careless laugh, and said:

"Oh, very well, if you don't like it; but you won't find my eyes look half the size they do now without it."

"I don't object to it in the least," I said,

pouring out the wine into her glass. "I only say, just now it is unwise. You can paint them as much as you like in Egypt. There the men and boys do it, and the women don't, so there you will be in the fashion again—the one thing that I think we agreed *was* necessary."

Theodora nodded and laughed.

"Now, do try to eat and drink something," I urged anxiously as the dinner was set upon the table.

The delicate colour came and went a little too readily in the cheek to please me, and the white hand trembled so that she could hardly raise her glass. As I was filling it for her the third or fourth time towards the close of dinner she pushed it from her.

"Don't, Cecil," she said in a low tone, "press me to take it, really."

"Why not?" I said chaffingly. "I thought Bacchus was your favourite deity."

"I never said that."

"Well, perhaps it's Eros then. Never mind, the two are very similar. Come, do have some more."

A Man's Life

"No; it will only make me more excited, and if you could know what I feel already——"

"What is it, my dearest?" I asked, suddenly growing grave and concerned, for she had put one hand to her left side and her face had grown paler than the marble table before us.

"Nothing—oh, nothing but the excitement—and all that."

The room had a good many people in it, though not in our immediate vicinity, and our table stood partially behind a screen. Still, though what we said could not be heard, our actions could be seen from the other end of the room, so that any demonstration of feeling was impossible. I could merely stretch out my hand and close it over hers that lay cold and lax and quivering on the table.

"Are you sorry to have entered upon this?" I said gently. "Are you afraid, after all, to trust yourself to me?"

"Oh no, not in the least sorry, nor in the least afraid," she answered with a sharp accent of intensity. "Only it is so difficult to make a man understand——" The carmine flowed

back to her cheeks again now, and she leaned
her head upon her other hand, so as to shut the
face from my eyes. I said nothing. I kept my
own firm, warm fingers closed over hers, and sat
in silence. I was distressed and anxious and
nervous for her health.

We had been travelling now for thirty hours,
and she had had no sleep for that time and very
little food, and a constant, ever-present excitement—an excitement, too, that dated farther
back than the thirty hours with me. For what
must her last night have been before she came
to me?—sleepless, at the least, as she had
confessed to me. Then there had been the
strain of getting away unobserved, and the
excitement and responsibility thrown upon her
by the new part she had to play. The mental
and physical strain and stimulus had been great
for a system so unusually easily excited to an ab-
normally high degree. I am a most utter egoist
as a rule—I know it quite well—but I do not
think any thought of self approached me then.
I loved Theodora intensely in those moments,
but the helpless weakness of physical nature

A Man's Life

appealed to me with tremendous force and kept the more selfish and the fiercer feelings in check. A tenderness towards herself was stirred suddenly by her visible, physical illness. A realisation came upon me of the fragility and uncertainty of these human lives, that when they are dear to us, we so lightly and so vainly call our own, and these two feelings helped to crush down the rage of my own personal passion and desire for her. I was willing in those moments to inflict any self-denial on myself. I was willing to repress and restrain myself to any extent for her sake, but I knew that this was the one sacrifice that a woman never forgives a man for making for her. I debated anxiously with myself as to what my duty towards her was, as to how I should, could, ought, must act within the next few minutes. The people were leaving the room, the waiters were clearing the tables and turning down superfluous gas-jets. I had not long to decide. It would have been an immense trial to me, an inexpressible effort, beyond all words, just then to have said to her, "You are over-

tired. Go and sleep, and forget me till to-
morrow;" but I would have forced myself to
say it—if I could have made clear at the same
time at what a cost to me it had been said.
But that was just what I could not do. If I
opened my lips to say the words, so harsh and
difficult for me, Theodora, like a woman,
would perhaps only go from me to a sleepless
night full of tears and distress, tortured by some
idea that I did not want her, by bitterly
wounded pride and shame that she had forced
herself on an unwilling lover. Peculiarly
between us the matter was delicate to touch,
because Theodora had come to me so voluntarily. My passion she had rather divined
than I expressed it. Action for the sake of our
love had hitherto, owing to our relative positions,
been on her side rather than on mine. That
we were here together now was the result of
her action, not mine. Had I not already
argued against her when she first came to me?
And how could she know, be convinced, that I
was in real and painful earnest, only speaking
and pleading for her and against myself?

A Man's Life

What if I still held myself from her? What would her feelings be? No man, I think, with a knowledge of the world and experience of women could fail to know the answer. It seemed to me now that, as it had been before, a certain amount of wrong towards her was forced upon me—an injury, slight or great, you may call it, according to your sensitiveness. Either now, when I saw she was unstrung and exhausted to the last degree, I must force fresh excitement on her, or I must inflict the mental pain of what might seem in our particular circumstances an insult. I felt I could not risk the last. I pressed the inert hand a little harder, and she suddenly let the other fall from her eyes and looked across at me. In those soft, uncertain, swimming eyes that sought mine, where the dark, tremulous pupil kept widening and dilating, there was a seductive appeal, an irresistible abandonment of self, a delicious invitation.

If my decision had been to resist, would it have stood now? As it was, there was no question: that seducing softness had been

147

Six Chapters of a Man's Life

thrown, half unconsciously perhaps, but half consciously, into the youthful eyes. I looked into them with a slight smile, and said, rising, as the waiter came up to clear the table and extinguish the gas, " Come."

CHAPTER V.

FIVE days had elapsed, and I was standing, looking absently through the coffee-room window towards the close of the afternoon, and thinking. I had left Theodora upstairs, lying full-length asleep upon the hearthrug before the fire. I had been already standing there some time considering these past five days, and trying vaguely to classify our tie, our life, and Theodora's position and title. I had never been in a more strange relationship with any human being before. Theodora was not my wife. In many senses she was not my mistress, a term which always carries a shade of disrespect with it. To her I might give, with greater justice, the tenderest name to me in the language, that of companion—a title so lightly used, but in its fullest sense so difficult to give and so rarely justified.

Theodora was now in every hour of my life, in every emotion, in my actions, and in my

149

thoughts, my companion, my associate, my comrade; and, as each of these, bound to me closer than any by the chains of the senses. Our relations were peculiar and heterodox, and my feelings towards her were inexplicably confused and contradictory, corresponding neither to those for the orthodox wife nor yet to the irregular position she was in. The relation, in so far as it was not marriage, was a derogatory one, or rather one which habitually becomes so, and in which we are accustomed to see women who are our inferiors; but Theodora was in a hundred ways, certainly in intellect and learning, mentally and psychologically, my superior. And for this reason it was impossible not to feel a constant, natural, spontaneous respect for her. But yet wide as the difference between wine and milk was the difference between the feelings with which I kissed her and those which men feel generally for virtuous women in the rank from which they take their wives.

For Theodora I was forced to feel respect. I could not do otherwise than look upon her as my equal or superior; but that reverence which

simplicity and innocence enjoins, that check-
ing, restraining constraint before ignorance was
entirely absent. In some men the constraint
inflames their passion, in others chills it. For
myself, excessive frigidity and purity in a woman
would always tempt me, not to seek her, but to
pass her by. If she is pure, let her remain so.
If I am to love my companion, that companion
must be my equal. If a woman considered herself to stand upon a higher moral platform
than myself, it would be wearisome and vexing
for me to be strung up to it ; at the same time
it would be a distress, and not a satisfaction, to
drag her down to mine. With Theodora there
was no constraint, no rein upon me ; not a bar
nor a shadow between us. With her, looks,
words, and actions were all free, unchecked,
spontaneous. I never tried, or felt bound to
try, to be better or different from what I was
naturally. From the beginning I took Theodora
without shame into my heart and brain and
thoughts, without their having been cleaned and
brushed up first for her reception. So that
afterwards I felt no fear that she might stumble

A Man's Life

some day on an unexpected rubbish-heap concealed in any corner. And Theodora came into my innermost life and admitted me into hers, equally without restraint. In the first days of our intimacy, the mental intimacy that between us immediately followed the physical, I was conscious of a certain shock, the shock of surprise, as she was so different from the average woman. It had passed, but it had been the birth of a fiercer, deeper passion. Nothing could exceed her cynicism. Nothing that I could bring forward for her condemnation, or say to excite her indignation from a moral point of view, did more than bring a curl to her flexible lip and a mocking smile into her eyes. Of every passion and emotion, of every desire and sensation that convulses the human brain, she seemed to have a theoretical knowledge, and a tolerance and an understanding for them all. She was ignorant of nothing theoretically, though she had had no experience of anything practically. And this mixture of innocence with knowledge, of physical purity with mental licence, fascinated me.

A Man's Life

Theodora stirred me as a narrow-minded woman could not have done. We met on equal, easy, broad, pleasant grounds, where the companionship and comradeship and friendship of a man to a man joined and met with and merged easily into passionate desire and the pleasures of sense ; and I felt—I don't say other men would feel—but I felt an infinitely stronger, more violent passion grow in me for this associate, this fellow-being, this co-thinker, and constant companion than I could possibly have done for any womanly wife.

Five days we had been here. And in those five days we had driven together and walked together, visited the brasseries together, smoked together, drunk together, played billiards together, and talked together. I possessed now a great friendship and a great passion—two things that come often at the same time in a life, but often, too, only the one to spoil the other. But here both were for the same object, and ran side by side, and yielded easily and smoothly, alternately the one to the other, unconsciously as our inclination led them.

When the friendship failed to satisfy, the passion rushed through it flaming and in-flaming; when the passion satiated, the friendship rested and soothed. It was a quaint, double position, with all sorts of various, varying feelings playing through it.

The fact that our real relations were known and suspected by none of the people that we came in contact with added another element of peculiarity, and had a certain irritating, stimulating charm. If there was no restraint, and the utmost freedom between us, ourselves, in reality and when alone, so there was an excessive and continuous restraint upon us both in public. An easy familiarity was of course permissible to our position as friends; but I had to keep a constant watch upon my words, looks, and actions, and be careful that they did not go beyond the elastic limits of friendship and excite comment and wonder. I did not grudge the trouble it gave me. I would not have had it otherwise, now I had once experienced the tremendous stimulus this restraint in public gave to our moments in private.

A Man's Life

Five days. Had I been married to Theodora in the orthodox way for those five days, and had the right and the opportunity of calling her "darling" every minute of them, probably my inclination to do so would have ceased by now, and a kiss between us have become as mechanical an action as putting sugar in one's tea. But since I could by no possibility address Theodora as "darling" except when absolutely alone with her and certain of no over-hearer, it was still a coveted liberty; while a legitimate kiss became a crime to be committed silently and secretly, with care lest we should be discovered, and as such retained its fascination. Even when the key was turned in the door of our room I used to be afraid lest Theodora's high falsetto voice should carry compromising words through the thin partitions on either side, and half of the delicious, intimate conversations we had had, had been carried on in whispers, broken by half-stifled laughter.

The clock behind me struck five, and I turned to go upstairs. She must have had a good long sleep by this time. When I entered

the room she was still lying on the rug, and
the fire had burned into a hollow cavern. I bent
over her. She was fast asleep, and I lifted
her up wholly into my arms without trouble.

Theodora was tall, certainly, but without any
great weight of flesh upon her. One could
not say she was thin, for all her bones were
so small and so hidden away in the smooth
limbs that it was impossible to find one, and
every joint and knuckle was only suggested
by a dimple. But round and soft as an
opossum as she was in this way, she was still
light and slight, made more like a very young
girl than a woman, without any ponderous
developments, and I could lift her up easily,
like a sleeping kitten. She stirred then, of
course, as I touched her, the heavy, white lids
quivered and opened, the lips curved into a
slow smile, and consciousness broke over the
face, like the sun rising over a landscape.

"Do you know you have been asleep three
hours?" I said, laughing. "I want you to
wake up now. We can have a cup of tea if
you like, and then we'll go out."

A Man's Life

"Have I really? three hours—what a time!" said Theodora, with a suppressed yawn and a smile in her eyes. "And what have you been doing?"

"I? Oh, I've been thinking," I said, throwing myself into the corner of the couch.

"Thinking! Great Scott! You don't say so! What an unusual occupation for a man! I never met a man who thought yet!"

"Oh, well, I do a lot of it, on and off," I said.

"Yes, I really think you do, and that's why I liked you so much from the very first. You are not a mere physical machine."

"Thanks," I said, laughing, and looking up at her as she stood in front of me. "You are very complimentary!"

"No, but really, Cecil, most men, young men, are such fools; either they have no brains or they will not use them," she answered, laughing too, and then added, "but what have you been thinking of?"

"Oh, lots of things," I said, looking into her eyes. "What does it matter? Come along downstairs."

Six Chapters of

We had tea in the empty coffee-room, and then went out. The weather had changed from cold to wet. It was mild and muggy, and the streets inches thick in mud. Theodora took my arm, and we kept step together over the dirty pavements. There was no ungainly twisting of her figure to hold up mud-stained skirts, no fussing about possible damage to petticoats, no dangling strips of torn braid or what not, that women are so fond of, to come flicking across the well-polished boots and disfigure the neat little feet that kept pace with mine. It was a charming young fellow that I had beside me, with the eyes of a woman. After a time we turned into a street that boasts the best of the semi-theatres, and we stopped before the doors of the building to read the boards. Everywhere was placarded the title of the first sketch—*La Joie Suprème.*

"Hullo," I said, "we may as well look in and see this, shall we? I daresay it will be amusing."

"What do they consider *La Joie Suprème*, I

A Man's Life

wonder?" murmured Theodora. "Very well, then, let's see. But, Cecil, I think our own opinion is pretty well fixed on the point for the present, isn't it?" with an arch and liquid smile.

I returned the smile and raised my shoulders.

"We can always take notes for the future," I said, and we went through with the little mob to get the tickets.

I had not the faintest idea of what we were to see. If I had had, I would rather have walked over the docks' edge with her than taken Theodora through the turnstile. I thought it was some variation upon the favourite pleasures of the French, and I knew Theodora had no ignorance and no illusions to be considered and bothered about. So we went in and took our seats in all innocence. My surprise and annoyance were intense when the scene rose upon a picture of domestic family life, and *La Joie Suprème* was proclaimed over and over again to be *La Maternité*. It was the representation of a woman who, having found dissatisfaction in many walks of life, at last settles down to a humble hearth, and as she rocks a baby in her arms tells the audience, amid thunders of delighted acclamations, that she has found no joy in life until now, in the kiss of her child and the rôle and duties of a mother! The very last play on the face of the earth that I would have brought my companion to.

Theodora's disguise, the sacrifice she had made for me, our life upon its present lines precluded all possibility of maternity for her, and the last thing I wished to do was to turn her thoughts and stir possible, slumbering instincts in that direction. I had not the remotest conception of what her feelings were actually, because I had dreaded and avoided the subject. She had laid down her rights to the ordinary life of a woman. She was apparently happy, and I would not for worlds have brought to her mind anything she might have lost by doing so. And now I had brought her to hear lauded, as the only virtue under heaven, the only sanctification of love, the one pure and lasting joy—Maternity!

A Man's Life

The French were enthusiastic; a really domestic nation at heart, and devoted to their
children, the play pleased them enormously.
The maudlin sentimentality and the high-flown
panegyrics upon wifely and motherly love were
received with unstinted clapping.

I sat silent, the blood hot in my face from
annoyance, and not caring to look at my companion. She sat silent and motionless too, absorbed in, and attentive to, this disgusting play.
What was she thinking? I wondered. Something of the old-fashioned idea that I think
most men have, that women are fond of
children and do covet their possession, and
the thought that Theodora was bitterly envying
this happy heroine before her, clung to me like
a wet blanket. At last, when, after three years
are supposed to have elapsed and in the finale,
this blest mother advanced to the footlights
dragging in one hand a little toddle in its
nightgown, saying, 'Voila l'auteur de mon âme
comme moi je suis l'auteur de son être,' the
house positively roared its pleasure, and in the
racket I ventured to look at Theodora. My

heart sank. As I thought: the splendid, smooth forehead was contracted and clouded. The high, narrow arch of the eyebrow was depressed with anger and discontent. She looked just as I had dreaded to see her looking, half resentful and half distressed. With the old-fashioned ideas crowding to my mind, and feeling awfully and genuinely sorry for her, I leaned towards her and said:

"Theodora, I swear I had no notion——"

"Oh, Cecil," she said, impulsively turning to me, "isn't it maddening? I don't understand this French half as well as I did that at the Concert des Ambassadeurs!"

For the minute I stared at her to see if she was genuine. No doubt of it. Then I flung myself back in my seat and burst out laughing. So she was only concerned about her knowledge! I had forgotten her intensely intellectual habit of mind.

"What are you laughing at?" she said, smiling. "I think it is very vexing."

"Oh, nothing," I said, while the French were still clapping, and the mother and the nightgowned infant still bowing their acknowledgments. "I say, Theo, what do you think of all this?"

"Oh, well, of course to me it all seems very idiotic," she said carelessly.

"Why to you? Don't you like children?"

"Like children!" returned Theodora in amaze, with her eyebrows lifted to her hair. "Why, Cecil——! No, I dislike them extremely. They bore me unutterably. I should detest the man who made me a mother!"

I was silent. It was an intense relief to me; and there was no doubt she was speaking naturally, and the truth. A sigh of gratitude escaped from my guilty breast, and I looked at the small, spirited head beside me, and thought according to the new canon, what does anything matter? I must get rid of all my old-fashioned ideas of women, that was very clear. I thought I had. Here five days with Theodora, and some still! A minute later a soft, caressing hand, sinuous, ingratiating, irresistible, came over the intervening fauteuil arm and touched mine.

"Cecil," she said in an undertone, as the noise was subsiding.

"What, dear?" I murmured back, ready to laugh again.

"Are you angry with me for what I said just this minute?"

"My sweet! No. Why should I be?" I answered.

"Oh, I don't know. Men are so priggish generally. They think if a woman does not rave about children she must be all that's vile."

"I am not one of those men then," I said, "and, under the circumstances, your tastes are extremely convenient."

"No, but Cecil, without satire——"

Theodora's face looked genuinely distressed now. She looked at me, the tremulous, beautiful pupil, with its half-unfolding, half-shrinking darkness, eclipsing almost the glittering, flashing iris.

"No, you little goose!" I murmured, laughing. "Surely you must know me by this time well enough for that! I don't care a hang for

children, and I certainly don't wish you to!
It's a rotten play; let's go."

After this bad shot I thought I owed Theodora some compensation, and when we got outside I made for the Café Bourret, one of the
best and brightest in the port.

"We want something to string our nerves
up, after all that fearful twaddle," I said.
"We'll dine here, and then have a game of
billiards, shall we, after? They have a very
decent billiard-room downstairs."

Theodora and I were both passionately fond
of billiards, and we had already played against
each other two evenings out of the five. I was
a fairly decent player, Theodora a downright
good one—as good a one as I have met amongst
amateurs, and it piqued and amused me to play
with her. Either way, whether I won or lost,
I was equally pleased. If I won, I had the
satisfaction of beating a better player than myself; if I lost, Theodora was my property, a
part of myself, and it was gratifying to me to
see the men who had watched our game press
round her and praise her strokes, as she stood

leaning her flushed cheek on the end of her cue. She assented to both my propositions, and we went into the café. There was a blaze of light, both gas and electric, a crowd of diners, and a continuous chatter going on all round that drowned the minor clatter of plates and knives. It was but the first piece that we had seen at the theatre, so that the hour for late diners had not gone by. All early ones, however, had disappeared, and we found a table without difficulty. Theodora's brilliant face attracted some admiring glances from the men as well as the women. Male good looks are rather at a discount in England, but as one moves southward and eastward their value mounts perceptibly. Theodora returned the men's glances with amusement, and I felt a certain jealous annoyance. At last, when the waiter had spoken twice to her without being able to get an answer, I said sharply:

"Can't you give your attention to the menu for a second, Theodore?" Theodora looked at me in surprise, laughed, and then gave her orders to the waiter. Then she said:

A Man's Life

"Now, Cecil, what are you cross about?"

"I am not cross. But why look back at these people as you do?"

"My glances are my own, and I shall do what I like with them. I hope you are not of a jealous disposition; it really gives too much trouble."

"You would not like it if I were indifferent!" I said, colouring with annoyance at her irritating, languid, contemptuous tones.

"No, of course not; but that is an absurd, sophistical reply. There are so many thousand ways in which a man can show his passion without making it the excuse for the tyranny of his own confounded jealousy."

Her face was so handsome at that moment, her voice so soft and caressing even over the last two words, such a warm light lay in the smiling eyes, that it neutralised the harshness they have upon paper.

"It is no use your being jealous of me," she continued lightly; "so don't begin it. Don't try it on, as the Americans say. It will only worry me to death and not change me. I am

not a little Hindu wife of eleven years old. I
have been free, perfectly my own mistress ever
since I can remember, and at close upon four-
and-twenty one is too old to make over one's
will to another person. I am your friend and
companion and equal, and you must treat me
as such; but you have half a knack of speaking
as if I were one of your Kashmeri women,
bought at a few hundred rupees."

I grew scarlet as she spoke.

"Theodore, what are you talking about?" I
said.

"No, Cecil, I daresay you are not conscious
of it yourself," she went on very softly and
gently, more as if she were persuading me to
give her something than finding fault with me.
"But, like all men, in these relations you are
confoundedly dictatorial at times, and I don't
like it. Besides, you have every possible thing
from me you want, and it's hard that you must
grudge a chance glance round a café."

She laughed as she ended, expanding her
scarlet lips into an intoxicating bow. I looked
at it and crushed any passing resentment at her

words. Was not all my pleasure just then in the hollow of her hand ?

I told her she was a darling, and should look wherever she pleased. We went on with our dinner, and Theodora confined her attention apparently to her plate. On her left, at the next table, sat a party of men, seemingly Englishmen, one of whom looked like a clergyman. They seemed much interested in us, and constantly looked in our direction. At last, towards the close of our dinner, and just as I had said I hoped all the billiard tables would not be taken, the clergyman leaned towards her chair and said:

"Monsieur is an Englishman, I believe ?"

Theodora looked at me, her eyes sparkling with laughter, and answered, "No, I cannot claim that honour."

"Oh really! You were speaking English so wonderfully well. Surely you are not a Frenchman ?"

"I think you will not be able to say what countryman I am," returned Theodora, looking at him and then at the other men at the same table. "Is it a matter of interest to you?"

"Oh, merely, I thought——" returned the clergyman hastily; "I was going to ask you to accept——" and he turned over a pile of pamphlets or tracts beside him in some confusion. "What persuasion are you?"

"The unpersuadable, I am afraid," said Theodora, mockingly.

I laughed, and leaned back and watched her. She made such a brilliant, animated picture. The young missionary was discomfited, but he persisted.

"High Church?"

"No, no church!" she answered, emptying the champagne bottle between our two glasses.

In his embarrassment her interlocutor failed to catch the word.

"Ah, Low Church," he replied hurriedly; "an Ecclesiastican?"

Theodora burst into a ringing laugh.

"No, an Elastican rather. Have you heard of that sect?"

A Man's Life

And then, amidst the laughter of the Englishmen who had caught the dialogue, she pushed
back her chair and said to me, "Come along,
Cecil; we shall lose our table."

When we got to the billiard-room the tables
were full, and there was nothing to do but
lounge at the bar at the end of the room and
drink. Theodora mixed her drinks recklessly,
but she seemed none the worse for them, and
when we got our table she played splendidly.
After that drinks and then another game, and
then more drinks, and then drinks, and then
drinks, and then drinks, and at twelve o'clock
we were both in that state when one ceases
to distinguish between the edge and back of
one's knife.

"No more, thanks; I have had enough,"
Theodora said decidedly as we stood at one
corner of the bar.

"I should have said that hours ago!" I said,
laughing.

"You should have said it? why didn't you then?
An obvious error on your part," she retorted.
"Well, at any rate, let's reel home now."

She purposely exaggerated, for we had not
reached the reeling stage. As the café closed
we walked out quite respectably, and strolled
with linked arms back to the hotel. The cold
night air did not increase our sobriety, and I
remember the hall porter eyed us sharply,
so perhaps we did not mount the stairs in
quite a straight line. Theodora and I, however, balanced each other, for we reached the
top without mishap, and going down the
corridor I thought how convenient and
pleasant it was to have that delicious figure
beside me, and that warm, little hand upon
my arm instead of a waiting wife who would
be uncomfortably cold to-night and uncomfortably hot at breakfast to-morrow. This was
a darling who looked none the less pretty for
a shade of intoxication, and who would be
none the less witty and intelligent to-morrow
for it, but who would not bore me with re-
proaches to listen to and excuses to make.
I don't recommend this kind of wife to other
men, I merely say I liked it, but then I am an
easy-going fellow.

A Man's Life

When we reached our door I gave her the key.

"I say, here's the key. Can you get it in?"

Theodora laughed.

"Now, Cecil, I like that! Why, I am as tossy as you are!"

The next day was Saturday. We got up very late, making our appearance in the coffee-room about noon; but as we had nothing in the world to do but to please ourselves, that did not matter. During *déjeûner* I told Theodora that I thought I ought to go and see a man connected with our company—it was a mere matter of courtesy, but still it was just as well that I should call upon him before leaving Marseilles.

"Oh, very well," she answered. "May I come too?"

"I think it would be better not. It might make talk perhaps, and lead to bother. You can amuse yourself without me for a time, eh?"

"Not so well as with you, but still I'll try. When are you coming back?"

"That's just what I can't say. The fellow lives in the Rue Plumier, outside Marseilles, I believe, somewhere in the suburbs. I may not be able to get back till late—midnight perhaps."

"But you won't be later than you can help, will you?"

"Now, do you suppose I should be later than I can help?" I returned jestingly, looking at her till the colour rose faintly under the soft skin.

I started in the afternoon, leaving Theodora playing billiards with one of the Frenchmen staying in the hotel. It was not quite the occupation I should have wished for her while I was gone, and I felt a jealous stab as I saw her commence the game. I was on the point of hurriedly exclaiming she might find something better to do, when it flashed upon me, what occupation should I prefer for her? The next instant I realised there was none that would give me satisfaction.

What I should practically like would be to leave her shut up alone in that dull, third-floor room with the key turned in the door till I came back. The unworthy selfishness of my phase of feeling came home to me so suddenly it staggered me. I saw for an instant into the heart of my egoism. I felt thoroughly ashamed of the impulse, and glad I had not spoken.

When Theodora said carelessly to me, as she saw me stand watching her, "You don't mind, Cecil?"

"Certainly not," I answered, and went out.

When I came back at two in the morning on the Sunday, out of the icy and deserted streets, I felt cold and tired, and as I climbed the six flights of stairs to the third floor I felt pleased to think I was not living alone. Visions of a room made bright to welcome me, and an expectant face to greet me, were in my mind. Some faint approach to quiet domesticity of feeling, to married orthodoxy came over me, a tranquil satisfaction and passion—barred. "Perhaps I shall become a reformed character, after all," I thought lightly to myself as I turned the handle and entered the room. Certainly it had all been made comfortable for my reception. A built-up fire blazed in the grate, curtains were drawn, the arm-chair wheeled up to the fender, the gas half turned down, and even the proverbial slippers, symbols of domesticity, lay by the hearth. But no Theodora! No waiting, wifely figure. No meek face with the patient, if slightly acerbus resignation of eight hours waiting on it. I looked round the room. Where the deuce could she be at this time in the morning? On the table lay, hastily flung down, the long-stemmed cherrywood pipe I had given her, and her tiny smoking fez beside it. The tassel swung rakishly over the edge of the table, as I was accustomed to see it swing over her white neck and ear. Feeling a strange transformation and reversion of sentiment, I flung myself into the chair to consider where I should seek her. What on earth could she be doing? I sent the domestic slippers flying with a kick as I stretched out my wet boots to the fire. Where was I to look for her? In the streets, in the adjoining night brasserie, or where? In what occupation, and with whom? Like drowsiness at the sting of a scorpion, so fled my feelings of sleepy fatigue, of mild languid content, and the chaste temperance of mind with which I came into the room. Wide awake now, I looked round the room, and my eyes fell on the male, fur-lined overcoat hanging on the door, the boots, similar to my own, lying under the chair, the small silk hat flung in the corner of the couch, and laughed at the thoughts they brought with them and at myself of a few minutes ago. "No chance of my reformation or decadence, whichever it is, into the domestic animal at present. By Gad, she is an education!" I muttered, the violent, two-edged passion I had for her stirring my frame as a sword might tickle one's throat.

I was annoyed, of course, at not finding her there; but the annoyance only stimulated a fierce desire to get her there. I had fully counted upon her being there; been absolutely confident, though half unconsciously so, of seeing a submissive, patient figure sitting at the fire, and had this been realised, the expected

greeting kiss would have warmed but not disturbed the fatigued and peaceful tenour of my
feelings.   But now, in the shock of her absence,
alone in this room, with these things of hers to
recall her position, all the keen, jealous emotions
of these relations broke into flame.   The
extreme insecurity of my possession came
home to me with sudden force.   The free
and perfect independence of my fellow stood
out well defined before me.   I had no legal,
no absolute, no apparent hold upon her.   There
was absolutely no tie nor bond between us,
except, indeed, that most sacred and most
blessed—of will.   So long as I stood first to
excite her passions and her fancies, so long was
Theodora bound to me, and so long only.   Had
our life been seven years old instead of seven
days, I might have quietly turned into bed and
left her to follow or not as she pleased; but
seven days is not the period for indifference,
and after the above stabbing reflections and
a few others I sprang to my feet in an angry,
irritated, excited flame of jealous passion.
"What the dickens can she be doing?" I

thought, replacing my hat, and I went out of
the room to search for her. The passage outside was unlighted, black and silent. The
whole hotel seemed wrapped in the profoundest
and most respectable slumber.

Undecided as to where to look for her, I
continued mechanically down the corridor, my
pulses beating faster and my thoughts growing
more angry every moment. I passed on, my
feet making no sound upon the carpeted floor,
meditating with myself whether I should go
and interview the night porter, when a streak
of light from beneath the end door in the
corridor caught my eyes, and almost at the
same moment I heard the sound of laughter
and voices coming from the same room, and
amongst them I could distinguish clearly
Theodora's high-pitched, effeminate, and somewhat affected tones. I stopped still for a second
as I heard them, the blood mounting to my
brain in furious waves. What were these
rooms? I knew they were all private ones.
The billiard, smoking, coffee, and reading rooms
were all on the first and ground floors. The

next moment I had reached the door and flung it open. Within, there was a blaze of light, and the air was full of tobacco smoke and the scent of brandy and liqueur. In the centre of the room, which was nothing but a large and well-furnished bedroom, stood a round table covered with green baize. Cards were scattered over it amongst the half-filled tumblers, straws, and toothpicks, and four men were seated at it—that is, three men and Theodora.

A game apparently had just been concluded. A gabble of French was going on. One of the players was leaning on the table and shaking an excited finger in Theodora's face as he shouted, " Mais si, mais si, on ne peut pas dire que l'amour et la fortune——"

She was sitting exactly opposite the door, and her head was leaning, yes, actually leaning, on her neighbour's shoulder. The veins in my forehead seemed ready to split as my eyes fell on her and saw her tossed dark hair and pale face against the fellow's sleeve. She raised her eyes, sparkling with animation, to the door as I opened it, and her eyes first met mine as I

came in. Whether mine revealed the rage of
jealous fury I felt I don't know, but as I looked
at her, I thought a shade of fear crossed her
face. The next moment the men had looked
round, and then with French courtesy one rose
and offered me a chair. "Entrez, entrez,
Monsieur. Asseyez vous," came from all of
them, and I could do nothing except enter
quietly and force a pleasant smile. None of
them were actually drunk, but all more or less
upon the border-ground.

I came up to the table and passed round to
Theodora's chair. Not even then did she alter
her attitude or remove her head from the
Frenchman's shoulder. I could say nothing.
I stood behind their chairs, beside myself with
the savage longing to seize Theodora and drag
her from the table and kick her companion
under it. He was a good-looking fellow of the
sleek-haired, smooth-shaven Parisian type, a
trifle older perhaps than myself.

"What time?" said Theodora, looking up at
me.

"A quarter to three," I answered, looking at

my watch. " Do you intend going to bed at all to-night, Theodore?" I said, looking at her.

Do what I would my voice shook with suppressed anger as I spoke, and the men looked from me to her with some surprise. Theodora rose hurriedly from the table. She staggered slightly, and I took her arm to keep her straight.

"Vous partez?" came a chorus from the trio with a note of keen disappointment.

"Mais oui, Messieurs, à trois heures il faut n'est ce pas?" she answered, with one of her most brilliant sparkling smiles. I gripped her arm tighter and dragged her to the door.

"À demain alors à demain, notre revanche," they shouted after us as I closed the door.

Without a word I hurried her down the passage, not heeding nor even hearing the few broken sentences she uttered. The passage was in utter darkness, but still it was public ground, and in public Theodora was nothing to me. It was when I had drawn her half shrinking and stumbling over the threshold of our own door that I took her into my arms

A Man's Life

and kissed her. I could not strike her, but my feelings were more akin to blows. I was conscious of nothing but a furious, intolerably stimulated rage of passion and jealous anger.

Theodora tried to wrench herself free from me with frightened efforts.

"What is the matter, Cecil?" she exclaimed; "are you mad?"

"Perhaps I am," I answered with a short laugh. "I think you are enough, Theodora, to drive any fellow mad."

"Now, Cecil, how unreasonable you are!" she said, still trying to tear herself away, with the tears in her eyes. "Let me go. You are hurting me."

"I don't care: you have hurt me considerably this evening!"

"Why? How? Surely playing cards is not a crime?"

"Playing cards! No," I said, with an all but irresistible desire to strike silent the insolent, smiling, wine and smoke-stained lips. "But when I come back at three in the morning I do not expect to find you half-drunk in another fellow's bedroom, with your arms round his neck!"

"Cecil, how can you be so unjust!" she said, "and do take your arm away, you will injure my throat!" with a burst of passionate, excited tears. "My arms were not round his neck, and as for the room, what objection could I make to that? If I were the man they think me, nominally there would be nothing in it."

"Well, there, hush!" I said, appeased by the rain of hot salt tears and the tremendous sobs that shook the slight excitable frame, feeling my anger rapidly sinking, engulfed and submerged in an overwhelming flood of desire. "But mind I won't have you enter their rooms on any consideration. Play, if you want to, downstairs, or if you can't do that, make some excuse and decline altogether. And why let them touch you? If you were fifty times a fellow, hang it, you know as well as I do, you could object to that. Surely you don't want them? You are not tired of me yet, Theo-

A Man's Life

dora?" I asked, looking into her still streaming eyes.

"Oh no, Cecil, you don't understand at all!" she said vehemently. "Only you were gone such an age—and you demand so much from me—perhaps you don't realise it, but this life has so much excitement in it; and then this eight hours—the reaction—they seemed eight years. I only went to find some—some——"

"And suppose, by chance, I had been detained and not come back at all to-night, what then?" I asked, reading a good deal between her broken, sobbing words.

"Oh, I don't know; I might have cut my throat. It is a state, Cecil," she continued passionately, "and you like it at times, and you can't complain of it at others. If I cared for you less when you were with me, I should be a safer person to leave in your absence."

The palms of her hands were burning; her eyes blazed through her tears, the dark lines of exhaustion showed beneath them; the scarlet lips quivered convulsively, and I felt every muscle in her tremble, and her heart beat hard upon mine. It was a question, as she said, of state and of temperament. And it is that intense crave and thirst after excitement, that peculiar, dangerous capability of excitement in another, that stirs it so strongly in ourselves. I thought I would not have her different, as I felt the electricity of the nervous frame pass through my own.

"No, I don't complain of anything," I said, pressing her closer to me. "Now, don't cry any more: kiss me, and let's make it up."

And that was my domestic home-coming! Through the following day, Sunday, Theodora seemed tired and quiet. We hardly spoke to each other through *déjeûner*, and I went downstairs soon after to the smoking-room, leaving her idling with a newspaper on the couch. Now, had this girl been merely my mistress, it would have been a considerable time before her presence again became so much of a necessity to me as to cause me to seek it. But Theodora was infinitely more to me than a mistress, and the foundations of her position

A Man's Life

were laid far deeper down in my necessities
and desires than those of a marriage or love
relationship. The passion for her sprang with
equal vigour from its twin roots, one of which
lay in the intellect and one in the senses.
Some may smile, perhaps, and say the last
only was real and the first but imaginary.
But I absolutely deny the impossibility of
that which one may term a passion of the
intellect, independent of the enjoyment of
sense — a passion which is born from the
delight that the presence of a particular
person confers, a certain peculiar pleasure in
their voice, in their language, in their movement near one or mere passive contiguity.
I admit that this intellectual or brain passion
rapidly suggests, and must inevitably give birth
to a sensual one, whether attainment to actual
possession of the object is possible or not.
But if possession is granted, it does not at all
follow that the brain passion is extinguished
in consequence; on the contrary, it then forms
the powerful living stem from which spring
incessantly the transient and short-lived flowers

of sensual desires. I admit also that this brain passion is rare, because it demands a great force of intellectuality in both the subject and the object, and in proportion as intellectuality and the impulses and requirements of intellect in man are rarer than sensuality and the impulses and requirements of sense, so is this brain passion rarer than that of the senses. But in natures where the intellect balances or more than balances the demands of the senses, and when these natures meet an object that delights the former and satisfies the latter, the bond between the two individuals becomes indestructible, and neither breaks nor frays in the strain of daily contact. This was the bond that existed between us. The instinctive pleasure and ease that I felt in her companionship underlay the keen attraction of her physical personality. But whereas the charm of the last varied and rose and fell with my own physical feelings, the first remained unchanged and possessed equal power over me in all my moods.

I wandered into the smoking-room, and stayed

A Man's Life

there ten minutes, heard some conversation that did not interest me, and then lounged through the billiard-room. Here a game was in progress, and I stood to watch it. There was a fellow near me also looking on, and I made some remarks to him upon the strokes. His answers were extremely foolish, I thought, and his knowledge of the game obviously nil. I walked on after a few seconds and entered the reading-room. Here I picked up some of the papers and read an article or two, yawned, laid them down, looked round, and, noticing a door at the other end, got up and walked to it. This led me into the drawing-room. It was fairly full, chiefly of women. One or two French couples were poring over time-tables or guide-books. Two or three women, minus companions, sat at side-tables. Several English and American girls were looking through the window or turning the leaves of a novel. I passed through the room slowly, as if undecided what to do, which I was, and several glances met mine and invited me towards particular chairs and tables. But, unscathed by the battery of eyes, I walked through the room and passed out at the other end.

The coffee-room was cheerless and empty. My feet carried me through it, and then instinctively took me to the bottom of the stairs, and I ascended them gladly to re-find her. I did not want the society of a wife nor a mistress, nor of any woman just then. I wanted a pleasant intimate, a sensible, intelligent chum, and I went to my present companion for these as confidently as I would have done for the former. She was intelligent, decidedly clever, and cleverness is the first essential in my eyes for a companion. I would tolerate and overlook moral and even physical defects, deformity, and hideousness, provided the intellect subjoined were compensatingly brilliant. She was curled round in the corner of the couch, fast asleep. I awoke her without ceremony. It was not till I heard her give a long-drawn sigh as she opened her eyes that it struck me it might have been more unselfish to have left her undisturbed.

"I say, I am sorry I woke you!" I said im-

A Man's Life

pulsively, as the dark wine-coloured eyes opened
upon me, which sounded a very senseless remark, but was true nevertheless, as I looked at
her.

People will quarrel with me for comparing
any eye to wine. But there was nothing that
those pupils and irides, when they seemed to
melt and mingle into each other in a dim light,
as now in this darkening room, reminded me of
so much. Their swimming, liquid, brilliant
depths, full of changing, varying lights and hues
and shadows, had just the mysterious darkness
and glowing warmth of wine seen in the shade.
They smiled on me now as wine flashes in a
sudden ray of light.

"Oh, don't be sorry! Couldn't find anything
to do downstairs?" she said lightly.

"No," I answered, drawing up an easy-chair
to the fire and lighting a cigar, feeling my
ennui dispelled at once, and a quiet satisfaction
diffused through me.

I found I had nothing particular to say to
her, nor she to me, but that did not matter.
The peculiarity of this strange, attractive influ-

ence that the society of some particular person can exert over the mind of another is its independence of the person's activity. Their absolute silence is as potent as their conversation. The charm acts, then, through our consciousness that if or when they do speak we shall be pleased and gratified, and our mind is quite satisfied with this confident expectation. The converse of this is equally striking. At any rate, I have found it so.

When shut up with a hopelessly unintellectual companion, his silence tortures me positively more than his speech. While he is talking the mind knows that it is suffering the worst that can be inflicted, and gathers a certain strength to bear the ordeal. But that terrible silence of a fool, when one's brain is kept in a momentary, agonised, nervous, semi-conscious apprehension of his next idiotic remark, which may be suspended over one's strained ears without falling for hours, is to me simply unendurable.

Perhaps I am particularly sensitive in this way, but if at times I suffer severely in consequence, I have still the compensation of hours

A Man's Life

like these, when the mere association of some
particular human being pours a delicious,
languid satisfaction like balm throughout the
entire mental and physical organisation.

We sat on, talking and silent by turns, and
the time slipped away unnoticed, till the room
was quite dark and full of the smoke from our
cigars, and it was with a feeling of regret that
we stirred at last and went down to dinner.

The day following we went on board.

Six Chapters of

Theodora and I had a lovely girl of about eighteen separating us. Her snow-white profile and well-dressed, canary-coloured head completely shut Theodora's from my sight. I tried to talk to her, for I heard Theodora's voice wholly occupied in a high rattle of French, gossiping with and chaffing the fat Parisienne on her other side, from whom I heard constantly the phrase, "Ah, mais c'est amusant ça!" The consequence was this pretty girl was left wholly to me, but she was atrociously dull. I got three whole sentences out of her besides "yeses" and "no's" during two hours.

It was a great relief when the women left the men to their coffee and liqueur, and hereupon I immediately moved into the pretty girl's chair, which brought me next Theodora, who was now discussing the quality of the cigars with the captain at the head of the table. As soon as I could get her attention I said reproachfully, "You have seriously injured my digestive organs by throwing the strain of that dreadful girl on me all dinner."

A Man's Life

Theodora turned her brilliant, sparkling face towards me and laughed.

"What ingratitude! That girl was sweetly pretty. I left her to you specially. You had a hideous creature on your right. I should like to have done the civil to that pretty girl; I thought you'd be enchanted."

"Pretty!" I said, stirring my coffee. "What is the good of a girl being pretty if she can't amuse you?"

"She was only a little shy," returned Theodora, turning two glasses of liqueur into her cup.

"Shy? well, Heaven protect me from girls who are shy then, if that is the form the disorder assumes!" I said.

After dinner I lingered a second or two in the saloon, looking into a novel on one of the tables. I could not have been more than three minutes, but when I went on deck I found the passengers had all resolved themselves into couples, and were already sauntering round the deck, two and two. I leaned against the rail smoking and looking for Theodora, thinking I would join her when I saw her. Then suddenly I caught sight of her coming down towards me, behind the other couples, and, to my disgust, she had the pretty girl with the canary hair leaning on her arm! I watched her, feeling a strange sensation—surely it could not be jealousy?—as I saw the straight, graceful figure revealed by the male dress coming towards me with an easy gait, the powerful shoulders and the small dark head bent down over her companion, who was looking up with a smile and a pink flush suffusing either cheek. Theodora was laughing as usual, and under a pretence of a slight rolling of the ship, she had drawn the girl's arm closely through her own. Her eyes were fixed in unveiled admiration on the wax-like face raised to her. As she passed me she gave a sideway, provoking glance at me, and the flash from under her dark lashes seemed to say mockingly, "I have woken up your shy girl, and I don't find her so dull."

They passed on. My eyes followed her till the perfect shoulders in the cloth coat were lost amongst the other figures, and then I

A Man's Life

turned and leaned over the vessel's side, and looked down into the water with a queer complex sensation that one might call mental dizziness. I could hardly find fault with Theodora now. Full of peremptory, jealous passion, I had dragged her away from the society of men when I had found her amongst them, therefore now this ought to be quite in accordance with my wishes. And yet, to see her making love to this girl set my brain in a savage whirl. I did not want to see her pass again, so I strolled down the deck towards the second-class saloon. A good-looking girl was sitting in a long chair, just outside it. I paused and asked her if she would stroll round with me.

"The vessel is rolling so much, I should lose my balance," she answered.

"Not if you take my arm," I said persuasively.

She got up, took my arm, and we mingled with the other strollers. We were now three couples behind Theodora and the yellow-haired girl. Theodora glanced back over her companion's head, and when she saw me she smiled and seemed well satisfied. I ground my teeth, and was so preoccupied I did not catch what the girl on my arm was saying. Then I made an effort and turned to her and flattered her and flirted with her and drew her out as much as it was possible—that is to say as far as she could come, but, like a cheap table drawer, that was not very far. Her conversation and all that she said was of no worth and full of no amusement in itself, as Theodora's generally was. And then the fact that she was extremely handsome was of no intrinsic benefit to me. I can never bring myself into the objective state of feeling. A pair of lips, however neatly turned, seem of no value whatever if I cannot or do not want to kiss them. Merely to admire them, unless indeed they are saying something to amuse me, becomes very wearisome. At last the girl said she was sea-sick. I blessed her constitution, and conducted her tenderly to the companion stairs. Then I looked round.

Theodora was sitting at the end of the vessel, still spooning with the yellow-haired girl.

A Man's Life

I went off to the smoking-room in dudgeon. At eleven I went down to the cabin. Theodora was not there, of course, and I took a few nervous turns in it, thinking, why did I feel so angry with her? Was it merely that I had wanted her for myself? I was very much in love with Theodora now, and any passion in me was apt to run to unwise extremes. But still, frankly admitting my selfish and jealous nature, there was an exasperating quality about her. It was a perpetual stimulus to my feelings in regard to her. There seemed no possibility of their settling down and remaining at any one respectable, moderate level. As soon as they were the least inclined to do so, she disturbed them all and threw them into a feverish confusion. And yet, was it not from this source that I drew my own keen moments of personal pleasure? Should I have cared a straw for a woman who offered me one tame, flat, calm, dreary level of content? I knew I should not.

A quarter of an hour passed, and then I heard a light step outside, and Theodora singing in

her aristocratic voice, which lent a dignity to
the words they hardly otherwise possessed—

> "Out all night, drunk all day,
> Lays me a thick 'un if I've a word to say—— "

The door opened.

"Oh, there you are, Cecil."

"Where the dickens have you been all this
time?" I asked.

"I have just seen Miss King to her cabin."

I consigned Miss King to another and a
warmer sphere. Theodora's face blanched as
she stood on the threshold.

"Come in and shut the door," I said per-
emptorily. "What do you think I am going
to do to you?"

"Don't know, I am sure," returned Theodora, coming in and closing the door behind
her, but not approaching me a step farther.
"You look cross enough for anything!"

I went up to her where she stood, with her
hands behind her, leaning against the wall,
her face looking excessively pale and strikingly
handsome in the glare of the two electric

A Man's Life

burners. I often wonder whether she ever felt actual physical fear of me as her changing colour seemed to show. I was several inches taller than she, being somewhere over six feet, and I was possessed of muscles that no amount of dissipation or Eastern fever could soften. She had pinched my arm once, and laughingly told me that I must remember that one blow from it would be enough to kill her. I rather incline to the idea that she had a certain fear, or at least felt that nervous excitement which in brave natures supplies the place of fear. But if she did feel it, it was not strong enough to restrain her careless, insubordinate spirit from saying and doing exactly what it pleased. And at times she was inconceivably insolent to me— an insolence that did little more than further inflame my love for her, not the tenderness of love, but—well, the rest. Perhaps she knew this, and deliberately used her insolence as she did other arts, but I think not; I think it was rather the outcome of her natural recklessness.

"What made you stick to that girl all the evening?" I asked.

"Why! did you want her? You told me you didn't," she said, wilfully misunderstanding me.

I made use of an impolite expression.

"Want her! Of course not! But what object have you in making love to another girl?"

"Simply to leave you free to do what you liked."

"Free to do what I liked! You know there was nothing for me to do!"

"Well, Cecil, there is as much for you to do as if I were not here at all, and a whole shipful of pretty girls dying to do the civil to you!"

"What are they to me?" I said impatiently. "What I want is yourself, and every one seems to have a prior claim on you than I."

"No, but look here; the thing is this. I can't bear that you should feel tied to me in any way. A man gets tired of anybody perpetually boxed up with him. If you had married me in the ordinary way, you would have had lots of change. You would have spent a great deal of time away from me. Then again, if I were a great friend or chum

you were travelling with, you would not be
bound to be always with me. I want you to
have as much freedom and as much variety as
you would have in either of these relations.
There can be no pleasure without liberty."

"Thanks for your consideration, but you
have given me a deuced lot too much liberty
to-night."

"Nonsense! you don't want me eternally
tacked to your side."

"Well, come along now," I concluded, knowing it was hopeless to try to vanquish her in an
argument. "I'm not ready to go to bed. We'll
get some pegs out of the steward, and then have
a stroll round. It's confoundedly hot down
here."

We went out together towards the saloon.
Although the sea was superficially smooth,
there was a great swell on, and the vessel
rolled heavily from side to side. Theodora
walked along the sloping, shelving boards with
firm, certain feet and beautifully balanced
figure that never lunged against me once, as
my recent companion's had done fifty times

in the length of the deck. And at last this independent security roused the contradictory desire in me that she should swerve and stagger and seek my aid and support. Then, as she did none of these things, the impulse to control these lithe, self-reliant movements became irresistible, and I put my arm round her waist and drew her violently against me. It was not an affectionate action, nor were my feelings the least affectionate, but it supplied a keen satisfaction to me, perhaps also to her. At any rate, she offered no resistance as I caught her hand and brought her own arm round me. She merely looked at me with raised eyebrows and murmured, " Remember, we may be seen."

" I don't care a straw about that," I answered, feeling that I was being perpetually denied my rights. " There is no law against our arms being round each other's waists."

A few steps more brought us to the saloon door, where a group of stewards or underlings of sorts were chattering to the stewardess. We went through them, and one of the men remarked—

A Man's Life

" Comme il est beau, ce petit là ! "

" N'est ce pas ? " returned the fat stewardess, sentimentally rolling up her eyes. " Ah, qu'il est ravissant ! "

This evening was fairly typical of all the evenings and days on board. I certainly could not complain that Theodora tried to mount guard over me as a piece of property belonging to her. She left me as perfectly unfettered as if she had been another fellow travelling with me. She never sought to be with me, to join me if I happened to be talking to the other passengers, or to stay beside me if others joined us. At the same time, to this reliance upon self, this independence, this freedom that she gave to me and took for herself, that scratched and kept awake my desire to attain to a more perfect possession of her, she added a flattering submission to me in public that gratified my vanity enormously. She was a distinct favourite with all the passengers from the minute we came on board.

There are some people who, from the strength of their individuality, seem to carve themselves out a distinct prominence in every society they happen to be in. At dinner the men liked to talk with her and engage her attention. In the smoking-room a knot invariably gathered round her. On deck the women fluttered and hovered round her, and her chair was always the centre round which the others formed up. And the general attention she received she turned into the means of a subtle flattery to myself.

To whomever she was talking, or whatever she was doing, if I came up and claimed her, she would break away with a careless excuse from her occupation and companions to join me—often to those companions' intense annoyance. The women must constantly have been "angered against me in their hearts." Constantly I used to find her sitting in the laziest of attitudes under the awning aft, with a court of girls and women surrounding her, and then my "Come and have a smoke, Theodore," was enough to make her get up and desert them, in spite of all their winning entreaties to "do just finish what you were saying, it was *so* interesting."

A Man's Life

On one occasion when I appeared in this way, the girl who was sitting next the conspicuous long chair, and with whom I suppose Theodora had been flirting outrageously, coloured to the roots of her hair as her lover rose obediently to my summons, and said furiously, " Really, Mr. Harrison, you seem to have no will of your own ! "

Before men her deference to me was quite as marked, and caused some comment amongst them. The same night at dinner, after the women had left, a discussion on the question of Protection arose between the captain and us at his end of the table. Theodora warmly defended it. The captain opposed it, and all the men near them took sides with one or the other. I listened in silence, principally because my French, though serviceable enough to get me through a dinner or light conversation, would be rather shaky under the strain of a political argument. The captain was French, and did not understand one word of English, and the same may be said of most of the parties to the discussion. This seemed to be no check to

Theodora; she gabbled off her arguments with perfect ease and precision. I stood it until she attacked one of my pet advantages of Free Trade; and then, summoning the best French I could, I broke sharply in upon her statement and ranged myself on the captain's side. Theodora turned to me. Her face was brimming over with the animation and glow of the argument. She flashed her eyes over my face, and then became suddenly silent, and no efforts of the men could get a further expression of opinion out of her.

"I decline to continue the argument any farther," she said merely when pressed to refute mine and the captain's view.

"We all know why that is," exclaimed the Parisian sitting opposite her with an angry sneer. "It's because you have found that Mr. Ray is on the other side!"

An appreciative laugh went round, and another added, "You don't dare to contradict him!" And a third put in, "Come, come, you have a right surely to your own opinion!"

I watched Theodora curiously, but she was

A Man's Life

not to be drawn. In answer to their raillery or their sneers she only repeated, "You may think what you please. I am tired of the discussion."

As she had been the liveliest supporter of it, it flagged after her withdrawal from it, and eventually fell to the ground. I rather enjoyed the situation. Perhaps I am peculiarly vain, but I am not sure that any other fellow would not have felt the same glow of gratification as I did at this obvious concession of personal rights to me from the best-looking and most brilliant individual present. Tibullus, writing of the male mind, could give no better advice to the would-be ensnarers of it than the significant hint,

"Obsequio plurima vincit amor."

Whether Theodora had ever read the line or not, she was mistress of the sentiment. And between her habitual flattery of my vanity and the perpetual excitation of my jealousy, those days on board did not tend towards calming my passion for her.

We came into Port Said early, about three in

the morning. Theodora and I were standing alone on deck. None of the other passengers had budged from their berths, but she was eager to see every port or station we stopped at, even for half-an-hour. And to gratify her I had been obliged to turn out reluctantly. A greyish haze that would soon be replaced by a pitiless blaze of sunlight hung over the flat, desolate, and sinister little port. It has, and justly, an evil name, and even at that time, when I had no terrible memory connected with it, it seemed to suggest its evil character to the eye. Its low, chimneyless, pink and yellow houses seem to grovel naked and ashamed of themselves upon the barren shore. No smoke rises from them. No tree grows near them. Round it lie the sands of the desert, that possess no eye to see nor voice to relate its doings. Over it stretches eternally an unchanging, pallid, argentiferous sky. While we looked across a stretch of grey water that divided us from it, and which the vessel was reducing each minute, the mails were brought on board. There was a letter for me, and I took it and tore it open, while Theodora was looking over my shoulder. I withheld nothing from her. She was accustomed to read all my letters, and had answered some before now. It would be perfect folly to allow such an intimacy to some women, but Theodora's feelings were above all wounding or surprising, and I concealed nothing from her in the present nor in the past, because it was simply quite unnecessary to. This letter was but a few scrawled words :—

"MY DEAR CIS,—Very down with fever. Shall soon have to toddle if this continues. If ship allows time, come and look me up for the sake of the old days.—Ever yours,

"JACK."

I saw the letter was dated from a Port Said agency of a London company. The handwriting was so excessively bad and faint that it was hardly legible.

"Theo, I think I must go and see this fellow when we land; I am afraid he is very seedy."

The warm, sympathetic eyes of the girl beside me lighted up at these words.

"Of course, if you like," she said simply.

Now, I had promised Theodora to drive her

into the native town, which lies back behind the port, and she had been very eager to see it, and, considering the vessel only halted two hours, we should not have time for both these things. To my promise, however, she made no allusion now, and she would not accept my apology under the circumstances.

"Don't be distressed, Cecil. It does not matter. Of course, your friend comes first."

So a quarter of an hour after landing we found ourselves in the dining-room of one of the matchbox-like houses adjoining the English agency. At the end of the room, under the window, through which came what sickly air there was, lay the slight, shrunken form of a man whom I had last seen as well as I was now. He got up with a smile and extended his hand, attenuated so that one seemed to see the light through it, and quivering like a leaf in the wind.

"This is awfully kind," he murmured as we shook hands, and then his eyes wandered curiously over my companion. I introduced the two, and then I sat down on Jack's couch.

A Man's Life

"What has knocked you up so?" I asked. "You look fearfully seedy."

"Nothing but this confounded fever. I can't get rid of it. The doctor gives me only three weeks now."

"Three weeks for what?" I asked, and yet knowing as I looked at him.

"Why, to live!" he returned with his familiar rackety laugh, but which now sent the scarlet blood flying over the white, emaciated face, and distended painfully the visible blue veins by the sunken temples.

"But, good heavens! Something must be done! You should get away for a change," I said.

He sighed enviously, and turned his gaze through the window.

"Change, yes! That's what I am dying for, but how can I get it? I must stick to my post here. I have not a penny except my pay. There is nobody to take over my work here for the agency while I go for a holiday. Besides, I have not the necessary cash for fares and all that. Oh, it's no use thinking of it," he added

215

hastily, as if to break off the subject, and with a glance at Theodora, "I don't want to worry you with my affairs. I did not know you would have any one with you, and when I heard the boat was coming in I thought I should just like to see you again before—before——"

His bloodless lips trembled violently, and he could not finish his sentence and looked away. Death is not a pleasant thing to contemplate at two-and-twenty. I was moved too. To me, full of life and strength and the triumphant pleasure of a gratified passion, the sudden sight of a fellow-being stricken and helpless, passing away from the world for the want of a few pounds or a friend to help him, appealed powerfully. A silence fell upon us all. I looked at him, thinking. I saw exactly what was wanted here, exactly what was the matter with him— continuous fever, that for weeks and weeks past had been eating away his flesh and strength until it had made him the wraith of a creature he was now, and that would return and return with greater violence, till under one of its gusts the weakened frame broke up and the life fled.

A Man's Life

This, if he stayed. On the other hand, a fortnight at sea, a change, a rest, time given for the
constitution to repair the damage done, and
the man was saved. I knew it, for I had seen
hundreds of similar cases. My impulse was at
once to give up my own passage and cabin on
board the boat and to let him go by it, while I
stayed and took over his work till he recovered.
I would have spoken out to him immediately,
as it all rushed through me, had I been alone,
but Theodora was with me, and to her I was
bound first. She stood to me before everything on earth. I glanced at her. Our eyes
met. I suppose she read my wishes. At any
rate she got up and came over to me, and we
both walked away to the second window at the
other end of the room.

"Cecil, if you want to take this man's place,"
she said simply without any preface, "and let
him go away, don't hesitate on my account; I
am quite willing."

"But the heat for you," I murmured, "and
your disappointment."

"Oh, you can't balance those things against

a man's life," she answered. "It will be an infinite pleasure if we save it. Tell him at once, for our time is limited."

I pressed her hand in thanks, and went back to the couch, leaving her at the window.

"You haven't any fever now, have you?" I asked.

"No; it always comes on later, after sunrise."

"Well then, old man, you've got to pick yourself up and go on board at once. There is our cabin, which is empty, and the passage is paid as far as Aden. So you must just trot along out there, and take three weeks' rest and leave me to mount guard here."

The thin face under my gaze went from white to scarlet, and then to white again.

"My dear Cecil, I wouldn't hear of such a thing!" he exclaimed. "I couldn't let you do it! When you have another fellow with you, too!"

"As to that, it is his suggestion," I said, laughing. "Come, you must not think twice about it. It's your only chance. It's lucky I

A Man's Life

have just turned up in time. Theodore will get all our things off the boat, and you must let me put you up what you will want to take with you. And if you give me an idea of what the work is and what there is to do, I'll promise to get through it all right. By the way, I don't know when you draw your pay, but you will want your expenses at Aden and your passage back. I'll give you a cheque on my bankers there."

And I got out my pocket-book and sat down at the table. Jack got on to his feet and came over to me.

"Cis, I can't accept it, really," he said, laying his all but transparent hand on the open cheque-book.

"Nonsense," I said, looking up. "Between us, what does it matter? Now, my dear boy, do be sensible. Fifty pounds is nothing, either way. I hope you won't be unkind enough to refuse it."

I dragged the book from under his hand and wrote the cheque, tore it out, and slipped it into his breast-pocket as he leaned across the table facing me. Then I put the cheque-book back out of sight before I called Theodora over to us, to set him more at his ease.

"Theodore, you would not mind going back to the ship, would you, and seeing the captain and getting off our luggage, or will all that be too much for you?" I said, looking at my watch. "I would go, but I must get Jack to show me his work."

"Oh, yes, I'll go," Theodora answered. "Bring the things back here, eh?"

Jack turned to Theodora with the nervous flush deepening all over his face and held out his hand. "Cecil says I owe this to you as much as himself. All I can say is, it's most awfully good of you both."

Theodora laughed gaily and shrugged her shoulders. "Oh, you must not thank me. It is his doing," she said.

They shook hands warmly, and she went out. The transfer of passengers and baggage was soon made. It is surprising how easy everything is to manage, provided only one is ready with unlimited tips and bestows them freely on

A Man's Life

all sides. By seven, before any of the passengers
had risen, Theodora and I stood upon the flat,
dirty sand of the canal bank and watched our
ship, with Jack leaning against the deck rail,
steam slowly out of Port Said. As we both
raised our hats in a final salute and turned back
towards one of the cafés for a cup of coffee,
not the faintest presage of ill-fortune was near
either of us. We both felt in the best of
spirits.

"What a sell for all those pretty girls on
board when they find they have left you
behind, Cecil! I am sure they thought you
would succumb to one of them in the end,"
Theodora said, laughing, as we were sitting in
front of a café facing the canal.

" Do you think so?" I said, raising my eyebrows. "I fancy it is you whom they will
regret the most!"

Our quarters at the agency were anything
but first-rate, and I could not help some stray,
longing regrets after my comfortable, hundred
guinea, four berth cabin. Theodora, however,
would not make the shadow of a complaint

against anything that had resulted from our change of plans, and with her figure moving in them and her brilliant face and voice seeming to fill them, I became resigned to the small, hot, dusty rooms. Our life for the next few weeks at Port Said was just such as one would foretell the life to be of two individuals in the first days of their passion for each other, who were sincere and ardent pleasure-seekers, unfettered by any prejudices, unweighted by any other ties, absolutely masters of themselves, with nothing but the lightest duties, entirely independent of any claim or consideration outside their own will of the hour, removed from outsiders, and only holding themselves responsible to each other for their actions. The result of this state would be more difficult to foretell, and would vary directly with the two individuals themselves. According to their natures, it might be satiety, discontent, degeneration, and a thousand other things. With us the gross result was the maximum of enjoyment that two human beings can supply to each other, and the net result was

A Man's Life

the highest degree of pleasure to both. At the same time, it does not at all follow that any two persons in our relations, and under our circumstances, should have attained this. On the contrary, as I have said, many, perhaps most people, would have found such a state end in misery at the worst, at the best in disgust.

Pleasure, the pursuit and preservation of it, is an art like any other. To enjoy living and the gifts of life perfectly needs an apprenticeship, previous practice, and natural talents thereto, just like any other trade, profession, or calling. It requires a certain training, as much so as bearing sorrow, enduring pain, being virtuous, and the like. It is quite a mistake to suppose that a man taken suddenly from sad circumstances and placed, free from any present trouble, under pleasure-giving conditions, will feel and be capable of feeling more satisfaction than a sunny-hearted individual accustomed to pleasure and versed in her ways. On the contrary, all sorrow leaves an ineradicable scar, and a long course of it eventually totally destroys the power to enjoy. Everything, if practised, becomes a habit, and nothing more thoroughly so than suffering or enjoying, and our temperament and all our capacities mould themselves to it, and whatever breaks in upon this habit and calls us into a state for which our temperament and capacities have grown unfitted is poorly and inefficiently carried out. The man whose habit is work cannot enjoy idleness for more than the shortest possible time. It *gênes* him far more quickly than the professed idler who gets through day upon day of it with the greatest ease. Similarly, the man whose habit is gloom, whose life has been, though it may not still be, melancholy, is unable to find, see, or taste amusement and diversion in the thousand and one things which give keen satisfaction to the born and bred pleasurist. The man of gloom lacks practice; his eye, from want of use and opportunity hitherto, cannot descry pleasure, lightly veiled in circumstances, though it is at his side. He would not know how to extract it or woo it forth, if he did descry it;

A Man's Life

he knows no methods. Could he descry it and extract it, he then would not know how to enhance it, how to dress it to his own particular taste. Finally, supposing by any chance he could descry, extract, and dress his pleasure, then still the great power would be wanting— he could not taste nor appreciate it; he is not a connoisseur. His own capacity, for want of training, is absent. Is there capacity in the farm labourer's palate to appreciate delicate wine?

For myself, I was skilled in the art of pleasure—a master in the profession of enjoying life. In my own life I had had no particular duties; no opportunities hardly, certainly no necessities for doing anything but providing my own amusement. I had had moments of great grief, despair, and agony, but still the habit of my mind was gaiety and the habit of my life ease. And being accustomed to both, I was adapted to both. Moreover, I was accustomed to my present relations with Theodora, for I had stood in them before to other women, as loved, though not more loved than she.

Six Chapters of

It is extremely foolish for a woman to wish—
if, indeed, she ever does, at any rate such I
believe is the idea—to be a man's first love. A
first love is generally some poor butterfly upon
which a man tries his raw and 'prentice hand,
with results disastrous in the end, and painful
in their evolution. Also he himself, through
his blundering inexperience, often secures but
the minimum of personal pleasure, and his
whole retrospect of the affair is full of shame
and irritation. The woman who comes fifth or
sixth at least should be thankful to the order of
her coming. Her lover has by this time gained
tact and dexterity in managing the whole
delicate, intricate, complicated machinery of
love, and she has the benefit of that perfection
of touch, that power to wield a passion, so that
it shall bring us the greatest possible pleasure
at the lowest possible price, in the attainment
of which the other poor, preceding butterflies
have been incidentally and unwittingly crushed.

Love is essentially a thing that requires the
help of art. To talk of two young beings
enjoying their first love, and to imagine Nature

A Man's Life

as a guide who will crown their love with
pleasure, is sentimental and pretty, but erroneous.
The two young beings generally secure for
themselves very little satisfaction out of it, as
indeed one might expect, since Nature has little
consideration for individuals and their pleasure.
Her interests are vested in the race, and to
individuals she is but an *ignis-fatuus*. If they
will follow her blindly, they must infallibly find
themselves sooner or later in the swamp of
disappointment. Our brains are given us to
defend and protect our personal interests and
supply our personal pleasures, which she would
ruthlessly push aside. In everything man must
supplement Nature by his brain before his own
satisfaction begins. Nature's bed is mother earth,
the breast of a damp and open field, but man
positively prefers his eider-down and linen.
Nature's food is the berry on the hedge and the
water in the brook, but man's pleasure is in caviar
and champagne. Why then, in love, should we
suppose for an instant that Nature's primitive
instinct in its simplest form can rival that same
instinct when moulded and fashioned and polished

by art and brought up through countless and minute evolutions to that artificial, complex, and ecstatic passion it can be in experienced hands?

This was the passion I could give to Theodora. She profited by my past errors, which I now knew how to avoid. In addition to this advantage, past experience reduces one's exactingness.

A pleasurist must be more or less a philosopher. Philosophy is a side branch of his profession of enjoying: he gets to know the worth of pleasure, the length of its duration, its inevitable reactions. Consequently none of these things shock him and shatter the constitution of his love as they do that of the tyro's. Knowing the exact worth of each satisfaction before he takes it, he has no disappointment after. Aware of its integral transitoriness, he feels no despair as it dies away. Familiar with the unavoidable reaction, he waits patiently for the, as certain, recrudescence.

The one great cause of the smoothness and ease of our relations was that I never expected impossibilities from Theodora. Her mental and physical weaknesses could not irritate nor annoy me. I had anticipated them from the beginning, and knew they were inevitable. Therefore they had no power to surprise nor anger. It was no effort to me to be lenient to them and overlook them. Similarly, with our passion itself, I never looked for it to bring unvarying satisfaction. In the very kernel of all passion are those qualities, the effects of which no art, no skill, no experience can wholly circumvent. Moments of tedium, irritation, reaction, revolt, for these there is no palliative but a smiling philosophy. It is useless to revenge ourselves for them upon our companion, who is no more responsible for them than we are.

Theodora in all this time had glorious health, and I took care that she should keep it. And side by side with the health and vigour that flowed through all the splendid, elastic, glowing frame, kept pace her inexhaustible gaiety and good spirits. Our life itself was pretty simple. Husmatrai, Jack's servant, brought us our breakfast somewhere between ten and eleven. From then till four the work of the agency occupied me, or at least supplied the necessity for my presence in the office. During those hours Theodora would sit in some corner near me, reading anything that came to hand, from Studies in Coptic to Zola's last. At four, coffee and cigars, a game of billiards, or a chat with other fellows who looked in. We dined at six. After that our horses were brought round— hired animals, but passable—and the rest of the evening and half the night we spent in the saddle; of course not invariably, but often, for the nights were tolerably cool and always brilliant after the suffocating dusty day. When disinclined to ride, we would go down on foot to the native town and ransack it from end to end in search of some amusement, which we generally managed to unearth in some form or other.

At the end of a fortnight I received a boyish, enthusiastic letter from Jack. He was cured, he was well. I had saved his life, and so on. In answer I wrote telling him to stay and confirm the improvement. And our life in Port Said flowed on, another easy period. Then the φθόνος θεῶν we had jested over in our first inter-

A Man's Life

view was realised. The envious gods struck
their blow. It crashed in upon me with terrific
suddenness, bringing the bitterest moments of
my life hard in upon the sweetest. I had
written again to Jack, giving him permission to
stay if he pleased, and the means of doing so.
The return mail from Aden brought me a
letter from him returning the last cheque, and
announcing that his passage was taken and he
would be back at the end of the week. I tossed
the letter over to Theodora when I had read
it, with the remark that we had better be
ready to leave on the day he arrived. The
same evening we went down after dinner to
the native city, seeking what we might devour
in the way of diversion. It was a hot, breathless night, yet not so hot but that I drew my
companion's arm through mine, and felt it
lean there with pleasure. The place seemed
unusually quiet this evening. We found
nothing to amuse us, and after a short stroll
we turned and went back through the city
towards the canal. It was just a mere chance
that, as we were passing one of the last native

buildings, a burst of tom-tom-ing reached us and caught Theodora's attention.

"That is the house it comes from, Cecil. Let us see what they are doing."

I looked over the house. It was a square, white, flat-roofed building, windowless in front, except for a few slits with rusty bars across. There was one door which seemed to open into an impenetrably dark passage beyond; over it flared a single oil-lamp swung on a stick, and some natives lounged at the mouth of the passage.

"I am sure the sound comes from the back there, and do you hear the laughing, too?" Theodora said. "Do let's see if we can go in, too!"

"I think we had better not," I answered. "Somehow I don't like the shut-up look of the place."

"Oh, that is probably only to avoid interference from the authorities. I think the house is all right. One never sees anything if one is afraid of everything. Do, Cecil, ask them if we can go in. Do, please."

A Man's Life

She pressed my arm and wrist close into her soft side and looked up at me, all the tender caressingness she was such a mistress of thrown into the handsome face. Now, I am always hopelessly, deplorably weak where the pleasure of another is concerned, and terribly open to the influence of an appealing voice and seducing touch. I cannot boast of that rigid inflexibility of dogmatic will towards others which many men think the proper thing to profess and possess. At the same time, it is to this weakness that I have owed chiefly, I believe, my success as a lover. The loved ones can tell quite well the sort of man with whom they will be likely to lead an easy existence. Intolerant myself of the least interference with my own will, I avoid, from a sort of fellow-feeling, trying to control, even where I have the power, the wills of others. Besides, to be frank, I was in the mood just then in which I could not have denied her anything. She saw it directly, and tightening her arm in mine she drew me over towards the door. I spoke to the Arabic-Egyptian boys standing there. No, it was not a public entertainment; it was quite private. There was no means of admission except by certain what they called "tikkats," which had been distributed seemingly by some indefinite person to other indefinite per‹ sons previously. We had no "tikkats"? Then by no possibility could we come in. I would have turned away on this pretext, but Theodora's eyes flashed upon me provokingly, as much as to say, "Not a single kiss shall you have to-night if you don't exert yourself more to please me." So I turned again to the boy, gave him a fifty piastre gold piece and told him to procure "tikkats," or let us in somehow. But he hesitated, not in taking the gold piece, but in letting us in, and mumbled something to his companions about the police.

"Oh, that is all right," I said. "We are not police. I am a company's agent here in the place of Mr. Gaisford."

At Jack's name the polished countenance of the Egyptian lighted up with pleasure, and in his enthusiasm he broke from the Arabic we had been speaking into English.

A Man's Life

" Gaisford sahib ?   Orr right ; orr right.   Me know Gaisford.   Jolly good chap !   Dear ole feller !   Often come here ! "

I raised my eyebrows and looked at Theodora with a laugh.

" So that is the way friend Jack gets through his money," I said to her, and then to the boy, " Well, never mind about Gaisford sahib.   If it's ' orr right,' let us in."

" First let master know.   You wait," he returned, and sidled away down the passage with a grin.

" I wonder what's on," I said to Theodora while we waited.   " Some dancing, I suppose, by the tom-toms.   Poor Jack ! no wonder he tries to amuse himself.   It must be dull work to live here alone."

After a minute a stately, portly Egyptian came down the passage.   He explained with profound salaams and great courtliness that there was no sort of entertainment, and positively no question of payment.   That there was simply a little dance, which was generally much appreciated by the gentlemen,

235

and to witness which he had invited some few personal friends. We were certainly welcome to make two of the audience, and free to bestow upon the dancer anything we pleased if he were so fortunate as to find favour in our honoured eyes.

"Oh, very good; I quite understand," I said when we had heard this formula, which was doubtless repeated to each stray unit of the public who sought admission; and then we followed him down the passage.

At the end of it ran up a few wooden stairs, which we ascended, the noise of the tom-toms growing more distinct every minute, and the sound of applause more defined. Our host pushed open some door in the darkness, and we entered an upper, back, and windowless room. The ceiling was very low, almost on our heads. The air was clouded with smoke, the light so dim that we could only just discern the indistinguishable forms of men sitting about on low benches or cushions, and we were led principally to know they were there by the murmur of applause going up on all sides. At one end

A Man's Life

of the room was stretched a crimson carpet, and on it was dancing a single figure, that of a youth of about seventeen. The light from a dozen lamps completely dark on all sides next the audience was wholly flung on the dancer. I heard Theodora draw in her breath as she looked. "Oh, Cecil, how lovely! What grace! I have never seen anything like it before." I laughed. So long as she was satisfied that was the main point. And I led her carefully amongst the benches and the squatting Egyptians to a front place. We sat down here on a low bench, just in front of the scarlet cloth. Theodora left her arm in mine, and her hand lay upon my wrist and pressed it every now and then in a sort of enthusiasm as her eyes followed the movements of the supple and exquisitely symmetrical form before us. We had entered near the termination of what one may call a figure, and after a few seconds the tom-toms ceased, and the dancer stood in the centre of the carpet, his smooth breast and throat heaving so that the chains and orna-ments upon it jingled, and each limb quivering

237

visibly with the strain. He was evidently a Levantine, white skinned, and of the true, supple, slender type. As he stood there with flushed face, and panting chest, and elated eyes before us, a storm of commendation rose from every side of the room, and handfuls of bronze and silver piastre pieces fell on the red cloth. Then he signified his intention of recommencing. A hush fell on the room, and in a fascinated silence the men were held soundless watching him. Such a dance, from its daring and ingenuity, from the marvellous agility and flexibility that it demanded, from the palpable strain and tension it put upon the powers of the human frame, must in itself have held the human eye excited and entranced, and here the singular beauty of the exponent rendered the excitement delirious, intoxicated. The men pressed round us as they closed in nearer the scarlet cloth, breath was indrawn, men scrambled up on our bench and lunged against us in the darkness. I remember distinctly every second, every sensation of those last minutes of pleasure that preceded the horrible afterwards.

A Man's Life

"You are pleased, darling?" I murmured to her.

"Oh yes, it's divine!" she whispered back in her excited way.

The tension in the onlookers became acute as the dance went on. The youth and beauty of the dancer roused us all, and a half shudder of sympathetic physical excitement passed through the room. Furious cries of "Bis, bis" came from all sides of it if the movements seemed flagging towards cessation. Gold piastre bits rained on to the vermilion square. I myself caught the enthusiasm and shouted "Bis, bis" strenuously with the rest. I flung my last handful of piastres towards his feet. They were chiefly silver coins, and as I had no more gold with me I drew off a ring and threw it into the circle of lamplight. Each time he attempted to pause we encouraged him with fresh shouts, and each new effort was watched in a tense and frenzied silence. It was evident, all the same, that the dance could not continue much longer without a break. We could see the sweat gleam on the dancer's throat, where the veins were swelling

into blue cords as he bent his smooth boneless
body double, backwards till the head rested on
the ground. He could not respond any longer
to the eager, disappointed, and brutal shouts
that urged him. A pallor suddenly overspread
his face, in spite of the paint upon it. He
staggered, quivered, and then fell senseless on
his face. The clamor in the room was deafen-
ing, and a rush was made towards the lamps.
Two or three Egyptians from an inner door, to
whom I suppose he belonged, picked him up
and carried him away, and raised the carpet,
literally covered with coins, by the four corners.
There was a good deal of confusion in the
semi-darkness. All the men talked excitedly
together, some scrambled over the benches and
went out: the room cleared rapidly. I looked
at Theodora. Her face was pale, and the tears
shone in her eyes; she leaned her head on my
shoulder with a burst of excited sobs. My own
feelings were roused by all that had just been
passing before our eyes, my own brain stimulated, and with this lovely and loved thing
beside me a sudden impulse stirred in all my

disordered senses. I put my arm round her and leaned over her and kissed her. It was a foolish, incautious thing to do in our position, and at such a time and place. The next minute I knew it. I looked up. Our Egyptian host was beside us. I saw him watching us through the gloom. As he met my eyes he drew back and disappeared. I glanced round us. In the dim, smoky room there were now only a few Egyptians, and they were going out stealthily like cats. We were being left alone. It was uncanny. A vague, undefined apprehension came upon me.

"I think these fellows mean mischief, Theodora," I said suddenly, as I watched them disappear. "We had better go."

"Nonsense," said Theodora; "it's all right. Take your arm away. Of course, if you will go on spooning me, we attract attention. That's all."

"It is not all," I insisted. "I feel sure there is something wrong. Come—you must come" —and I got up hastily and laid my hand on her shoulder.

"What a fellow you are, Cecil!" she answered, looking up with a smile.

However, she got up, and we made our way out from amongst the benches unhindered. We reached the head of the little wooden staircase and stumbled down to the passage where we had entered, and by the light of the tin oil-lamp flaring against the wall we saw that the door was no longer open, but shut.

The red painted wood shut out the dark square of midnight sky, and four massive-limbed Egyptians lounged with their backs against it, bending against their hips their Port Said knives. Involuntarily our feet stopped, chained at the lowest stair. Theodora was just behind me. I glanced at her, and saw she had read the situation. "Trapped," she said laconically, without a change of colour. Unconsciously my hand went to seek my revolver. Theodora noted the action and seized my arm.

"It's folly," she said hurriedly. "Two against four, and forty more behind. For God's sake, don't show the revolver; they will

A Man's Life

simply cut us down. Besides, we may want it for ourselves later on."

Even in that moment a throb of admiration went through me dully at her words—so cool, so careless, so indifferent, so unfeminine, as always.

"Speak to them. No insult, no force. Bribery, conciliation. Our lives are in our tongues, Cecil," and she laughed.

As for me, my blood seemed freezing in my veins. I had a pretty clear presage of what was coming.

"Unbar the door," I said to the nearest Egyptian.

He drew his knife from his hip and held it idly, point towards his shoulder. The slightest turn of his wrist now, the least impetus, would have brought the curved blade whirling to my throat.

"The order has been given to detain you," he answered, and his eyes were fixed on Theodora.

"What for?" I asked quietly.

"You may go if you please, but your companion remains with us," he returned.

243

Theodora stood silent beside me. The other Egyptians stood silent, impassive, looking on.

"But why?" I asked in my calmest voice, feeling every drop of Saxon blood in my body turn into boiling lava with fury and revolted loathing and rage. I knew, I knew all already. Why did I not turn and shoot her then?

"Our master is very sick, and he hears that he," and he pointed an authoritative finger at Theodora, "cures sick people. He wants him to stay and cure him."

"You infernal liar!" I said, unheeding Theodora's appealing hand on my arm. "You know your master is not sick. Unbar the door for us. We represent a Government, though we are only two. Your whole house can be razed to-morrow if you detain us against our will."

The Egyptian looked at me and then at the cornice above his head, playing with the handle of his knife in silence. He neither stirred nor answered. Theodora stepped forward and laid her hand with a supplicating gesture on his sash—the scarlet roll of silk

244

knotted above his hips. I sickened as I saw her.

"Where is your master?" she said, in the same soft voice she used to her lover. "Is he very ill? How long do you want me to stay?"

The Egyptian looked down upon her graciously.

"We would entertain you for a week. At the end of that time you are free to go whither you will. Meanwhile, your friend may go; we have no need of him. At the same time, let him remember," and he looked at me over Theodora's shoulder, upon which he laid his hand, "if he appeals to his Government, and tries to rescue you during that time, your life pays forfeit. In your blood he razes this house."

Theodora nodded. Her calmness was unbroken—her face like a stone mask.

"And you would let him go? Now? At once?" she said; "and myself at the end of the week?"

"As there is one God and no other."

We spoke to the man in his dialect.

Theodora now turned to me and said in English, "Cecil, there is no help for it. You had better go before they change their minds."

"Theodora, you are mad!" I said desperately, my heart seeming to fail more at her words than those even of the Egyptian. "What are you saying? Leave you here! Don't you understand what they mean?"

Her eyes met mine, full of the familiar light and power, and with a laugh in them.

"Is it likely that I don't understand?" she said. "Of course I understand. But I also understand the situation. What terms can we make? Look here, I see the whole thing. We shall not be able to move these men, they are rocks. They have seen you kiss me. We have betrayed ourselves. Nothing now will satisfy them but——" and she shrugged her shoulders, "or our lives."

"Then it shall be our lives," I said shortly, drawing her to me with a hand she could not resist, and putting the other to my side.

Theodora looked past me at the Egyptian.

A Man's Life

"Give us a few minutes in private," she said appealingly, "and I will persuade him to leave me."

The Egyptian silently drew aside a thick black chick that swung on the left wall of the passage and revealed a small, dimly-lighted room beyond. He motioned us to go in, and dropped the heavy chick behind us. The moment we were on the other side of it Theodora flung her arms round my neck in a wild burst of sobbing tears.

"Oh, Cecil, you won't kill me, surely?" she pleaded, and I felt her warm tears on my neck. "You have always been so kind to me; you won't have the heart to do it. Think what it is to shoot me!"

She had her own soft, small hand upon mine that held the revolver, and she kissed me on the mouth between her words. I stood motionless, unmoved by her, feeling only the fury within me. In those moments I had only one instinct, one thought, the murderous desire to kill her. It leaped up through me, pervaded me, and swayed and bent my whole mind and

body, involved them in itself. I felt no tenderness, no pity, no remembrance of love.
These were obliterated, annihilated in the
savage, mindless, brutal lust to kill, this impulse which lies so closely curled round the roots
of every lover's passion that only our reason
divides the two. I longed to destroy her now,
as I had once longed to possess her, to shatter
and burst those eyeballs and blot out their light
for ever, to lay open the temples and transform
them into a shapeless bleeding mass, to keep
her mine now as I had made her mine then.
To check those quick heart-beats, to see the
veins drain out their blood, and the whole
malleable body grow damp and pulseless, would
have been to me now the keenest, supremest
pleasure, surpassing even the ultimate moment
of possession. Theodora saw it all printed
upon my face, and she clung to my hand beside herself with terror.

"Speak to me, Cecil."

"You value your life above your honour,
then?"

"Infinitely," she returned cynically, her face

pale as that of a corpse already, and her eyes suddenly blazing with mockery and contempt.

"I do not, then," I said in a low tone, my hand clasping tightly the revolver.

"I daresay!" answered Theodora, and the light, scornful tone cut through my brain like a knife. "My honour! A convenient term for the preservation to yourself and your own egotistical, jealous, tyrannical passion, of this flesh and blood. Think what our life has been! Cecil, you accepted me for your own desires as Theodora; you can't now, for those same desires, turn me into a Lucretia!"

The clear, rapid words fell upon me from those pale, scornful lips like so many sword-strokes. My brain seemed to rock as I heard her. Was it not true what she said? Was it anything but the unsparing truth that she stabbed me with? What was this instinct to kill her? This impulse to accept death for us both rather than another should touch my property? Was it noble? was it pure?

Rather was it not, as she said, but another development, another phase of the passion and the desires of the flesh. Too much, too much we love the body and too little the mind, which cannot be defiled. It was the lithe figure and the full throat and the flexible hand that had struck away the revolver; it was these things that swayed before my disordered senses and maddened them. Those lips that I had known I would rather see mutilated and blackened, streaming with blood from my own hand, than know they had been pressed, smiling, by another.

Is this a lofty and honourable instinct? Through and through my tortured brain passed like lightning the scorching questions. Yet women for this word "honour" have been slain over and over, and their slayers sung. But what is it, this slaying, but a gratification of self? My fingers quivered on the revolver.

"Theodora, do you care for me so little that you can submit——"

"My dearest one!" broke in Theodora, the words pouring from her lips in a passionate, unbroken stream. "I care for you so much

that I won't throw away your life for an idea.
Sacrifice your life at eight-and-twenty for a
woman's honour! Great God, what is honour?
What is your standard? who is to judge between us? Have we not long ago done with
all laws and put our own intellects in their
place? This is not a thing of choice, it is
necessity. To χρῆν, Cecil, το χρῆν," and her
fingers clenched like steel upon my wrist.
"You know I care for you. I have done
enough surely in proof—— Do you think that
I stay here willingly? It's unworthy of us
both, the thought. The degradation! Bah!
we shall both survive. You know, you must
know, I would not suffer it at any other price
than this—our lives. Is my mind and my soul
and my will that they cannot touch—are these
nothing to you? The friend and the comrade
I have been to you, you will throw away, because you are asked to lend the mistress! It
will be agony, Cecil, to let you go and to
remain here, but there will be hope, certainty
of re-union with you. If you kill me, all is
over. There can be no union for us amongst

the dust and worms. Think! There is no hereafter! Death is only the coward's refuge. I would rather meet what is to be met. I would rather live and endure and come out of this den into life again than drag you with me into a grave. Still, if you wish—shoot!" and she raised my hand and the revolver, on a level with her mouth. "Now, murder the woman you profess to love! Come!" she said mockingly. "Make haste! You have only a few minutes!" as I stood transfixed. "You have had all from me. Now take my life!"

In that horrible moment her face burned itself indelibly into my brain. Look where I will now in my sleepless nights, I see it still. The lips, that were close to the revolver's muzzle, wore the old cynical, reckless smile. The eyes, full of their male, taunting, unholy fire, glanced unflinchingly down the barrel. Her words paralysed me. What was I to decide her destiny? Was I to set my will above another human being's? What right had I? Was I to become a tyrant, simply because I had been

252

A Man's Life

a lover? I had had all from Theodora. True, but all had been given me. I had asked, and she had granted. I had never bent or broken her will to mine. It was my nature to shrink from forcing another, and tyranny of any kind I loathed.

"No," I said mechanically, "I cannot take it if you will not give it;" and I slipped the revolver back to its place.

A tremor, a sort of convulsion passed over Theodora's frame, and she threw herself into my arms. All her body burned against me, as we strained each other, breast to breast, her hands clasped my throat like bands of hot iron, her lips on mine seemed drawing out the life. It was a passionate, fearful embrace, that clings to me still in my dreams.

"Kiss me. It is the last time."

And I kissed her. Better, infinitely, to have passed from that frenzy into death, if she would but have consented. What does it matter when one has lived whether it be two or twenty years, twenty or forty?

The chick at the side of the room was burst

aside before I had released her. The men, some nine of them, pressed into it.

My arms sank like stone. My own instincts were beaten down, as they had been before, many times for her sake. I set her free. The precious moments in which we might have secured our release had gone. I had conquered myself, and we both lived to suffer. Four of the men seized my arms and led me to the door. Five of them closed round Theodora.

"Cecil," her voice came to me full of an intolerable anguish, " good——"

The word perhaps was " Good-bye," but the last syllable never reached my ears. It was cut short at her lips, whether by a kiss or a blow I could not say. But that appeal to me sent a superhuman strength through me. The fury of loathing and hatred seething in every vein lent me an irresistible force. I turned my head back to her and wrenched my arm free from the Egyptian on my right, and a blow from it hurled him against the wall. The next instant there was a flash across my eyes, a tremendous stroke across my forehead, and

A Man's Life

then all sense glided away under the inrushing darkness.

When sense came back to me, I was lying in the sand of the roadway. All round me there reigned absolute silence. The moon had risen and threw its light along the quiet road; over me loomed the wall of the house as I lay on the edge of its shadow. I rose giddily and unsteadily, brushing the blood that had flowed from the forehead away from my eyes, and looked over the blank windowless walls, feeling as if my brain would burst with agony as the flood of sentient consciousness rushed back upon it. The white walls in the moonlight glared back upon me till they seemed to spin and reel in my strained vision. Then I began to walk—walk as the tiger does in his ten-foot cage. Up to the edge of the shadow of the house my feet mechanically carried me, and then back again. What could I do? My thoughts seemed driving through my head, like two-edged knives, tearing as they went. To rouse the authorities and invoke their aid would result in what? Before that house could be forced or razed or burned, before any European hand could reach the inmates, there would be ample time for them to revenge themselves upon their hostage and evade retribution for themselves by some easy death, and to me the officers of justice would render back a mangled corpse. In my hand I held her fate, and the knowledge of this weighted me, chained me to inaction.

Inaction! inaction! In that blind thirst for vengeance, in that rage of anger, in that mad longing to regain her, it was the cruellest torture that could be inflicted. But inaction it must be. She had begged her life of me, bought it now at the highest price, and it still lay insecure, uncertain in my keeping. I was its treasurer. Had the malignant spirit which seemed to have pursued me with reference to this woman, and transformed, antagonistically to myself, even my least selfish actions into positive transgressions against her, determined also to make me the destroyer of her life itself? The nails sank deep into my palms. There was nothing, nothing for me to do but to wait,

256

A Man's Life

to suffer, and to submit.   Mechanically I took
out the revolver.   It shone in the white light.   I
looked at it with a delirious desire to shoot
myself through the eyes.   Its bullets in my
brain would be more welcome than my
thoughts.

Bah! What was death that she should have
escaped it at such a cost?   Obeying the
wild craving for obliteration—obliteration of
memory and of thought, the insensate longing
for a blank, a nothingness, a powerlessness to
think, my fingers cocked the revolver, and
then I undid their action with a dreary laugh.
I was fettered to life, just as I was fettered to
passivity, for her sake.   Where could Theodora
turn, if not to me, when they released her?   I
thrust the revolver back out of my sight.   She
would return to me, and I must be there to
receive her back.   To take my own life, upon
which hers depended, was but a form and a
manner of taking hers.   I walked on and then
back, on and then back, under the wall, as hour
after hour of that night went by, oblivious of
everything, insensible to everything, in a hell of

self-reproach and of insane, useless, powerless rage. At last the twilight warned me it was getting near the dawn. To be seen there by natives or Europeans, to excite suspicion, to draw attention upon the Egyptians, to allow any information to reach indirectly the ear of the law, would be as fatal as to seek its aid. The light was a peremptory summons for me to withdraw.

In the grey morning I turned away from the house and walked eastwards and homewards, leaving her there. I reached my own house, unfastened the door, and went up the stairs. In a dazed and disordered way I yet felt keenly that all Theodora's safety rested on my actions, and with some instinct working for me, more allied to the madman's cunning than reason's fore-thought, I crossed towards the glass. I saw my hair was matted with blood and filled with sand. The cut itself was high up, over the temple, and concealed by the hair; so much the better. There was blood upon my face and upon my shoulder. In an hour's time I had changed all my clothes, washed away the blood,

A Man's Life

and descended the stairs. At the foot I met our servant. He stared at me in dismay.

"Allah, have mercy! The sahib is ill!"

"Yes, I am not well. Bring me a cup of coffee and some brandy," I answered, and passed on into the dining-room.

I sat down, with my arms outstretched before me, staring into vacancy. Was it credible that I was her lover and yet acting like this? Conniving at the whole matter, actually sheltering her injurers, preserving their immunity from discovery? Mockery, bitter mockery and irony and derision of fate that forced me to act, look, feel like her murderer, this same fate that had forced me before, while determined for her own sake not to become this woman's husband, to instead become her lover.

"Will the other sahib return to breakfast?" inquired the man, re-entering.

"No; nor will he rejoin me for a week," I returned. "I expect him to come back here at the end of that time. Husmatrai, here," I added, as he turned to go. "No talk. Do you understand? Silence." I looked at Husmatrai,

and he bowed to the ground, striking his forehead many times with his hand, murmured
"The sahib's slave," and withdrew. I did not
in the least anticipate that the tale of my companion's absence would go any further than
ourselves through his agency. I knew the man
liked me, and I had always treated him well.
The secret was safe, the murderer might feel
secure, I thought to myself, with the shadow of
a bitter smile as I walked to the desk by the
window and turned over the correspondence.
There were two letters that had to be answered
at once. It seemed to me I could never bend
my mind to them. I had to read each through
half-a-dozen times, but at last I realised their
drift and wrote the replies. Then there was a
lengthy report to be looked through concerning
the shipping in the Canal, full of errors that it
was my business to correct before it was printed.
The figures jumped before my eyes, and the lines
of writing wavered up and down until I thought
I was losing all control over the swimming
brain. The events of the past night rose before
me with remorseless persistency. A hundred

A Man's Life

times my thoughts travelled over the same
ground. A hundred times I was descending
that wooden staircase to the closed door.
Wherever I looked—on the walls, beyond the
window, on the paper before me—I saw Theodora standing with her hand on the Egyptian's
sash.

It was late in the afternoon before I had
finished all the work and left it ready on the
desk for Husmatrai to despatch. I called him
in and sent him away with it. Then I turned
and went upstairs. Fever was beginning to
burn in every fibre and cell of my body; I felt
I must lie down. As I entered the room and
crossed to the bed my eyes fell upon Theodora's
handkerchief lying there, and the yellow paper
novel she had been reading the previous afternoon. A sudden, terrible realisation of irre-
parable loss rushed in upon me, an overwhelming
sense of irremediable, immeasurable injury. I
flung myself face downwards on the bed and
drew her handkerchief under my lips and kissed
it in a passion of uncontrollable sobbing.

Every night of those seven I went down to

the native city, and remained within watching distance of the house till dawn. I gained nothing. There was no sign, no sound. Those blank white walls and narrow slits behind their aged, rusty bars told no tales. The door beneath was shut now. There was no light above it. Not a single being passed in or out.

Whatever my term of life may be, whatever I may have to suffer, there can hardly be more pain in store for me than was crushed into those seven nights, while I waited and watched under the wall till sunrise, alone with my thoughts. The one great pulse that beat savagely through them all was anger against her—a bitter, implacable anger that she had rejected death by our own hands.

At times, wrapped up in my egoism, in my entire thought of self, which is the base of all men's love, I felt I did not care whether she returned to me living or not. To burn, raze, sack this house, to drag out the hounds that skulked there, to avenge myself on them, and then shoot myself on her corpse—this was my most present desire. If she did return to

A Man's Life

me living, then what ? The angry blood flooded
all my face and my brain seemed bursting open
under the question, but still I loved her well
enough to know the answer. I could not desert
one who had given up so much for me, been so
much to me, as she had. Mere honour—at
least my notion of it—would prevent me.
Theodora was as certainly my future wife at
this minute as she had been when I had first
consented to take her with me. If she did not
return at the end of those seven days—then for
my vengeance.

The moonlight fell in liquid silver along the
sand, my dogcart stood at a little distance, and
I paced, with my own black shadow for company, up and down one short length of dust
from where I could see the house. It was the
seventh night. Much more of this and my
brain must have lost its balance. Suddenly, as
my straining eyes were fixed upon the door, it
opened, a shoot of lamplight—and a slight
figure was thrust out that stumbled and fell in
the sand. The next second it had risen, and
Theodora fled towards me down the moonlit

road. I held out my arms to her, but she avoided them, and the next second she was at my feet in the dust, convulsed in an agony of sobs, each one of which seemed as if tearing the life from her.

"Oh, Cecil, Cecil, it would have been better had you shot me as you wished."

We had changed, for I thought not, as I leaned down and raised her in my arms. This human thing in which still centred my desires. Her head strained violently back over my arm, so as to keep the face from my eyes; but they sought it, and the moonlight fell full upon it. Good God! it was horrible; blotted and covered with sores.

"Oh, I have lost you! I know I have lost you! You won't care for me now." And the wild, bloodshot eyes met mine in an agony of unutterable, intolerable shame.

She was fearful to look at in that moment, but all sense of loathing or repulsion, the recollection of personal loss, every trace of personal resentment, was suddenly carried away, swept from me by an overpowering tide of pity for her. Every voice within me was struck silent by the despairing misery, the imprint of frightful suffering upon the disfigured face. No thought of self could live in the tremendous sea of sympathy and distress for her that seemed to roll through me as I looked upon her, and, moved only by one great impulse to soothe and comfort her, I bent down and kissed her lips. It was the purest kiss I had ever given her, not the kiss of passion nor of personal pleasure, but the kiss of consolation. It was the highest, noblest, most worthy moment in all the course of our passion—this moment when Theodora was to me neither wife nor mistress, but simply a loved fellow human being. That which I had striven vaguely to attain and had not, in the flush of pleasure and the satisfaction of the senses, I had gained now in pain and shame, and when she came back to me disfigured and degraded—I loved unselfishly.

As the clinging slough from the lizard, my own desire fell from me in that moment, and unblinded, unweighted by it, I was free to love her as a human being should be loved, in and for itself, not for the joy it may confer upon another, but absolutely, for itself only, as approaching and relating to divinity. Now at last, when my passion was held paralysed and revolted in my veins, when Theodora was no longer lovely and desirable to me, when all my senses turned from her, stricken with loathing, it was then that I knew and could claim that I loved her in the truest, highest meaning of the word. Now when I had nothing to gain from her, when there was no thought of pleasure or gratification for me, when I ceased to look upon her as an object of delight for myself, then first most truly I might be said to love. Her words, " Oh, you won't care for me now," cut through me like the blow of a knife; they seemed to lay open my own heart before my eyes, to reveal to me the worthlessness and baseness of the love I had for her—if those words were true. Had she known and accepted with resignation the thought that all she possessed was the vain, fleeting desire of the flesh, and that with a blot upon the beauty, a stain upon the purity, it must vanish ?

A Man's Life

Evidently: and her words smote me with tremendous force. So had I been loving her, so had I proved my love for her, that in a moment like this, of abasement and humiliation, she should turn from me in hopeless, helpless terror, willing rather to face death than her lover, if her beauty and her virtue, the sources of his pleasure, were destroyed. A dull self-reproach, a dim realisation of the intense egoism of men's love, filled me, as I felt the weak, strengthless form flutter and try to escape from me and hide its agony and shame and pain anywhere but in my arms. The man to whom she had given all she possessed while she possessed it, was now in her misery to be fled from, one from whom no tolerance, no sympathy could be hoped or expected. I drew her closer into my heart. My anger against her was dead. Every emotion was lost in the mere longing to comfort her, to diminish this distress I was witness to, to lift off from her some of this burden of shame that seemed crushing her.

Effeminacy, weak-mindedness, my forgiveness

of her may be called: very good: I can bear the stigma of effeminate weakness better than I could the torturing thought that I had added one touch of pain to another's degradation and despair. I murmured some words of consolation, but to deaf ears; I felt her collapse suddenly, her head sink heavily on my arm, and I saw she had fainted. In this state I lifted her into the dogcart, took my seat beside her, and drove back to the European quarter.

It was a night of horror that followed. It was not till I had carried her into the house upstairs to our room and laid her on the bed that she recovered consciousness, and then only to pass from it immediately into delirium. All night long she raved, and I had to listen, pacing to and fro at the foot of the bed. Slowly the time crept by, minute by minute, marked only by the inflections of that strained, sharp voice. The house was still, silent, containing only our two selves. The window stood wide open, showing the broad, sandy road to the canal. It seemed as if the dawn

A Man's Life

would never break behind it. From time to time Theodora would raise herself in a fit of terror and try to fling herself from the bed. Twice it was as much as I could do to save her from throwing herself headlong to the ground, and then when she felt herself controlled she would burst into a frenzy of delirious shrieks that echoed through the empty rooms. Each word she uttered in these paroxysms seemed to fall on me like a drop of molten lead into a wound; for this terror that oppressed and haunted her — what was it? It was almost wholly a terror of myself, the fear of meeting me again. The horror that loomed before the sick, wounded brain and drove it from its balance was really her lover's face. To escape from that, to kill herself rather than come back to me, was the string upon which hung and jangled all the other broken thoughts. In all her raving the same theme recurred incessantly, the certainty that I should condemn her, the certainty that no pity and no mercy could be expected from me.

With the morning the fever lessened. When the light fully filled the room I bent over her and saw she was conscious. Motionless, speechless, on the verge of coma, she lay with closed lids, her face colourless except for the crimson and livid patches of the sores. She opened her eyes under mine, and then, as they met my gaze, a terrified, shrinking anguish shot into them and the lids closed again, as if to shut out the sight of some horror-striking object.

"Cecil," she said, before I had time to speak, "am I very much disfigured?"

"Disfigured! No! and, Theodora——" I said with an uncontrollable, desperate longing to vindicate myself, "if you were ten thousand times disfigured you would be the same to me!"

Theodora made no answer. The shadow of a sceptical smile curved the pale, weak lips. She was in a state of collapse, and I felt it was not the time for argument and protestation I persuaded her to take some soup, supporting her head on my arm; then, as a tinge of colour came to her cheek, I asked her how she felt.

270

A Man's Life

"Nothing much, except intensely weak," she answered, and I could hear the weakness in her voice.

I sat thinking. The boat left that afternoon. Would it be well to urge her to make an effort to leave by it, or would the exertion be too much for her strength? Jack would be back that night or to-morrow: we could go. The chances of recovery on board ship, with the sea air to breathe, were greater than here in this stagnant, unwholesome air of the port, and the change of place, the removal of these hateful associations, would be an infinite relief to the mind. At the same time the movement and fatigue and excitement of starting would inevitably bring on a new access of fever. Sitting thinking of these things, her voice suddenly startled me.

"Cecil," and her hand touched my arm that rested on the counterpane, "you were so anxious to marry me once. Will you care to marry me now when we go home?"

She turned her head slightly towards me, I closed my hand spasmodically upon hers.

271

"Of course I will marry you!—at any time, the first moment we can do so, here or at home."

She gave a faint laugh.

"Well, it is of no consequence! I shall not trouble you."

I could not answer her. There was a burning in my throat and a mist before my eyes. But her words determined me to risk everything to get her away from this accursed port and its memories. When I had found my voice I pressed her to get up and try to leave with me that day. Theodora rose with a painful effort, sat up and brought her feet to the ground, pretty, tiny feet, so small that both could almost lie in my hand. I could not prevent her tottering over to the long glass standing in the window. I was close beside her and supported her with my arm, or I think she would have fallen as she caught sight of her own image. As it was she staggered and almost slid from me.

"Good heavens, Cecil, how my face is swollen! What is it? How awful! I could

272

not recognise myself, and my hair, too; look at it!" She passed one hand over the little black silky head I loved, as she spoke, and a shower of hair fell to the ground. "What a sight I am! utterly hideous!"

I wondered it did not strike her how lovely the figure was that the glass gave back to her as it leaned against me, how beautiful that solid white neck, set between those perfect shoulders, as the cold morning light struck upon it, where the linen lay partly open on her chest. I told her my thoughts, and added—

"Now come! don't worry about your looks any more. You will get them all back."

"You are a dear, charming fellow, Cecil— you always were, and I am so sorry to make you look so ill and worried," she answered, and turned from the glass.

I offered her a chair, but she sat down on the floor to put her shoes on, as a child does. That toilet was a trial to us both. She evidently felt frightfully ill, though she made no complaint. Her hands burned like the actual touch of flame. Every movement was so weak and uncertain that I dreaded a fall at each moment. As she dressed I could hear the bones of her wrists and ankles, sucked dry by the fever, crack and snap with painful distinctness. She forced herself with unflagging courage, but her fingers and her limbs trembled so excessively that each simplest action took three times its normal length of time. At last she was dressed and sank upon one of the chairs by the window —sank as if she would never rise again. She looked at me and forced a faint smile.

"Now I am all right. Go and make any arrangements that may be necessary, and come back and fetch me when you are ready."

I went out, down to the quay, keeping my thoughts fixed resolutely on the immediate present. Just then I did not dare to think of either the past or the future. The steamer was in when I reached the canal shore, and I took one of the boats to it. There was an air of fresh life from end to end of it when I stepped on deck, a mass of women's light dresses grouped on it aft; the sound of laughter and conversation making a murmur under the

awning. It all struck heavily upon me as I
made my way to headquarters. I engaged two
passages as far as Aden, taking a small cabin
at the extreme end of the ship with but two
berths in it, the only one vacant, found out
that the steamer left an hour hence, and then
hurried off it back to Theodora.

When, three quarters of an hour later, in
the full glare of an Egyptian noonday, we drove
down to the canal together, the fever had
mounted four degrees, and she was on the
borders of delirium. She talked a little wildly,
and her voice was unnaturally high and strained;
she was perfectly clear at present and sensible
of what was said to her, but I could see that
it would not be for long. The long flight of
steep, slippery steps that form the ship's ladder
down to the boat is an instrument of torture to
any one stricken with fever; and the look that
she cast upon it as we neared the ship went
to my heart. Over the side of the vessel
and round the head of the ladder leaned an
idle crowd of the first-class passengers, for
whom, in the *ennui* and monotony of ship life,

a boat approaching from the port becomes an object of interest. The bright, light dresses of the women caught the sunlight, their scarlet sunshades, balanced over their heads as they leaned forward, blazed in it, their gloved hands held the rail, and their laughter and chaff reached us in the boat. I saw a crimson flood of colour pour over Theodora's distorted face as she glanced up.

We went up the steps side by side, under the gaze of about forty curious eyes, very slowly, for fever robs the muscles and the bones of power to move, except stiffly and with intense difficulty. One of her trembling, scorching hands lay on my arm, the other on the wooden hand-rail. When at last we reached the top, the captain himself came hastily forward through the passengers before we had set our feet on the deck, and, looking at Theodora, said nervously something about "contagion" and "the other passengers."

"I assure you there is nothing contagious," I said; "but if you feel afraid we will consider ourselves isolated to our own cabin until he

has recovered. I feel sure a few days at sea
will set him straight. If not, put us ashore at
Ismailia: I believe you touch there?"

"Well, gentlemen, of course if you keep to
your own cabin—otherwise—really—the responsibility——"

"Certainly," I answered, and after a second's
hesitation he stepped aside and let us pass on
deck.

The well-dressed, idling crowd divided and fell
back before us as if we were brandishing red-
hot irons, and murmurs reached our ears from
every side: "Disgraceful," "Ought not to be
allowed," "Leprosy," "Small-pox," "Looks as
if he were dying," and so on. I did not heed.
I was too much engrossed in noticing the
increasing heat and pressure of my darling's
arm to think of anything else. When we
reached our own cabin Theodora relinquished
her hold upon me and threw herself into the
lower berth and let her head fall heavily towards the wall. The next time I spoke to her
she had lost consciousness, and answered me
incoherently. I shot the bolt on the cabin

door, and then sat down on the couch under the window.

Thought, terrible thought, the relentless pursuer of man, rushed in upon me, and I could not escape from it. We were leaving the port then, and no vengeance had been taken. And yet what worth is vengeance when it can undo nothing? I glanced at the incomparable figure, lying with bent head and collapsed limbs, and ground my teeth down upon my lip till the blood started violently. The low, raving voice filled the silence of the cabin; from above came down across it at intervals the light laughter of the women upon deck. Within my own brain there seemed some terrific tension, a cord stretched and threatening to snap at each instant. Fearfully and bitterly had Fate mocked my jealousy— mine, I who had hated a chance glance upon her . . .! A knock came at the cabin door.

"Who is it?" I asked.

I felt as if I could strike dead any one who addressed me at that moment.

"The doctor."

278

A Man's Life

I got up and opened the door.

"I heard some one was ill, and thought I could be of some assistance to you. Do you want anything?"

"Yes," I answered. "You may bring me some antifebrine in five-grain packets by preference. And order the steward to bring a series of cups of tea, as hot as he can manage; and, look here, say it must not be the filth one generally has for tea on board. Tell him I'll give him half-a-guinea a cup for each one that's drinkable, and—doctor, come in a minute," I added, and he came inside.

I put my arm under Theodora's head and turned her face towards the light.

"Now, you see what these sores are. They are the ordinary Egyptian sore, contracted by drinking impure water or something of the sort. They are not contagious from one to the other in the ordinary sense; so, for Heaven's sake, disabuse the passengers of the idea. He will never get well down here; I want to get him upon deck."

"No, no; of course they are not catching

279

through the air; I'll tell them all that. But they are through contact, mind; and I'd advise you to touch him as little as possible." Then he added reflectively, "It's a very grave case of fever—very."

"Grave! I know it is; but I think it's only severe simple fever."

We stood silent a second listening to the half-inarticulate, delirious muttering from the burned and swollen lips.

"Couldn't say, I'm sure," he returned. "Looks to me as if there was a touch of brain about it. What is this 'Cecil' he keeps repeating?"

"That is my name," I said with a flush.

"Oh, ah! I see. Well, we must note how things go. I'll let you have the febrine at once," and he went out.

The heat in the cabin was suffocating. As the ship lay our port was southwards, and the sun's rays poured into it. The new white paint with which the cabin was lined, blistered and cracked, and filled the few feet of air with its stifling odour of lead. The flies from off the

A Man's Life

land swarmed in through the port-window,
settling upon and clinging to everything, and
all my efforts were only just sufficient to ward
them off her face. There was a continuous
hurrying of feet and dragging of chains and mer-
chandise past our door, and a tramping backwards and forwards overhead, with every now
and then a crash of some bale of goods over-
turned or thrown down, at which Theodora
would start up and stare wildly at me. From
the canal came the scent of stagnant water
putrefying under the sun's rays; from the
body of the ship that of rancid oil upon hot
iron, and these strove for predominance with
the paint, in the thick heated air.

When one is on deck, where one generally is
while a steamer is loading or unloading at an
Eastern port, the tumult and the noise is hardly
noticed in the movement of the scene; but shut
down below decks, under the low roof of a tiny
cabin, one seems in the centre of a very pande-
monium of clamour, heat, and stench. The
vessel was late in leaving, and to me, watching
her full of desperate anxiety, the minutes passed

like centuries. At last, at three in the afternoon, we were moving, and began to steam
slowly down the canal. The afternoon wore
away, and then came a rush of orange light
flowing into our cabin and filling it at sunset.
This faded into a gradual obscurity, and I
lighted the tin oil lamp on the wall, and the
evening went by as the afternoon. Theodora
lay in a silent stupor. The steward came at
intervals, otherwise I saw no one. At ten
o'clock the doctor came again.

"It's all right now; you are at liberty to go
up on deck," he said. "I have told them there
is no danger. How's your friend?"

"About the same, I think," I answered.

"Well, come upstairs for a time yourself;
you really should."

"I can't leave him now; the fever has just
come on again," I said hastily.

"Did they send you any dinner?"

"No, but it's of no consequence. One can't
eat in an atmosphere like this. Thanks, all the
same."

"I'm going to have a smoke up aloft. Mind,

A Man's Life

if you want anything in the night, my cabin's close here."

"Thanks," I said; "good-night," and I went back to her.

For six days and nights I was with her incessantly, and a slow, steady improvement in her state became clearer day by day. On the sixth, at midnight, when we were nearing Aden, I was sitting up with her, watching her. She was better, the fever had subsided, the temperature was lower. There was every hope. The tremendous weight of fear that had been crushing and chilling my heart under it was lifted off me, and a soothing, peaceful calm stole through me, as I sat and watched her. Her head had sunk a little sideways on the raised pillows; the dim cabin lamp sent its light fully across her features. The vile sores had died off the face; there was no mark of them visible in this light. Pale, bloodless, and calm, like a carved ivory image, she lay there, as motionless and apparently as breathless. The face was the same, and yet how changed from the countenance I had been watching for the last terrible six days!

As the livid, moist sores and scabs had died from the smooth skin, so had the distress and the strained anguish, and the imprint of suffering fled from the whole face. The unspeaking lids concealed the pained, excited, glittering eyes; the tremulous, fever-burned mouth quivered no longer. Both the pale lips were folded together in peace, and the old sweetness had come back to them. I looked and I felt nothing but a supreme and infinite thankfulness. Never at any time had she seemed as dear to me as now. A little after midnight she opened her eyes, and they encountered mine upon her.

"Cecil!" I crossed to her berth and stood by it. "I believe I am much better, and shall live now; but in case anything should happen, I want you always to remember you have nothing to reproach yourself with. You have been most kind and good to me. You will remember."

I flung myself on my knees and put my arms round her and kissed her, on her neck, between her chin and bosom. "Why should you say such a thing?" I asked passionately.

A Man's Life

"Nothing will happen. I won't let it. You are going to live now."

"Oh, yes. I know I am," she answered, with the familiar, jesting levity, as she twisted her soft arms round my neck and leaned her head against me. "But still, I want to tell you you have been very good to me, and—I love you."

It was the first time this phrase had ever passed her lips. I had not missed it hitherto in our relations, but now I knew suddenly I had not heard it from her before. Perhaps her innate, indestructible self-knowledge had barred her utterance of it until now. What had existed between us up to this time? Love? Rather an unlimited passion. Almost immediately she had spoken her eyes closed, her arms loosened and unclasped. I reined in my own emotions, and let her head slide gently back upon the pillow. The least excitement now would bring back the fever. A few moments after she seemed to be asleep. It was intensely still. Within and without the cabin not a sound disturbed the silence;

there was not even the lap of water against the ship's side. Beyond the port-window, the large, square glass of which I had set open to its fullest extent, I could see now one constellation, in the dark space of sky, then later another, while the first had disappeared. This marked our passage; otherwise, in the stillness at this end of the ship, we hardly seemed moving. Silence and heat seemed brooding upon everything, and they seemed to press upon me like a stifling weight.

For eight nights I had had no sleep, and between excitement, anxiety, and fear I had not missed it. The slight fever in my own body, besides the strain on the mind, had warded it off from me and kept me through the whole time strung to the highest pitch of wakefulness. That peculiar, keen wakefulness, that sharpened clearness of the brain and an utter absence of fatigue that tropical fever supplies to a man as no drug can supply, had been mine. But now, as I felt the palms of my hands, they were cool, the fever had left me. The danger seemed to have passed for

A Man's Life

her, and with it the tension upon me, and now suddenly, sitting in the silent cabin, with her serene, sleeping, ivory-hued face before me, my own exhaustion came down upon me like a black, whirling cloud. Suddenly I felt I must sleep. My arms dropped. My head sank. The cabin rocked, and then faded into darkness before my eyes. Sleep, sleep. The next minute I had staggered to my feet with a start. I was there to watch her, not to sleep. It was quite possible the temperature might rise and the delirium return towards morning, and in the delirium she had already more than once tried to throw away her life. I forced my lids open, but they seemed like clinging lead. I steadied myself against the edge of the berth and looked at my watch. Nearly three. But three more hours, and then another watcher could be found and I could sleep—yes, sleep—sleep on for hours and hours, but now I must keep it from me. I looked round the cabin, but there was nothing amongst all those bottles but sedatives. Even as I looked at the shelf where they stood

it swayed, and my lids fell over my eyes. With
an inconceivable effort I tore them open. How
could I keep myself awake? Motion was
denied me, for there were but two feet of clear
space in the cabin. Every muscle, every limb
seemed collapsing. Throughout my whole
frame there was the one urgent, peremptory
order of nature—sleep. The intense longing
for it drowned and obliterated every other
thought and sensation. It crept upon me, the
vile, physical weakness; the drowsiness grew
thicker and thicker over my brain, and my
senses, lying upon them like fold upon fold of
a suffocating blanket. It was nonsense that I
could not conquer it—I must. I stumbled
across to the window to get the outer air. My
feet seemed wrapped in cotton wool, the
muscles no longer held the lids up from my
eyes. I saw dimly the ledge of the port-hole
frame and clutched it. A breath of cooler air
came to me off the salt water, but it came as
from a long distance, unreal and indistinct; it
could not rouse me. I was sinking into this
utter night of black unconsciousness. The ex-

A Man's Life

cessive physical desire, like some vast, actual
hand, the Hand of Nature, gripped me. It
came upon me, and seemed to bend my
shoulders and thrust down my head till it
sank upon my arms. Then dimly I saw my
penknife lying on the ledge. In the confused
and failing brain, the idea came slowly, painfully, struggling through the mists of sleep—
a cut. . . . Yes, a cut—pain roused one. The
penknife was open, and my inert, heavy fingers
closed upon it. I drew it unsteadily across my
left wrist with my eyes half shut. I tried to
press it hard, but it seemed to me like wool in
my fingers. I felt vaguely a burning on my
wrist, and the mist before my eyes went into a
sea of red and scarlet—that was all. Then
thicker than before came down the black,
blinding curtain, my head sank to some rest-
ing-place, a divine, ineffable relaxation passed
through every fibre. Softly, like oil poured
into the open wound, flowed over me the tremendous satisfaction of the tremendous longing,
and—I slept. After a time a dream came. I
thought Theodora was sitting up in the berth

looking at me and gesticulating and talking, but none of the words reached me. "The delirium has come back," I thought, and I strove to get over to her, but my feet were weighted to the floor. Then I saw her scramble from the berth and approach me; her eyes blazed upon me. I tried to find my voice, but I struggled to speak, vainly. Her lips were moving, but I heard no sound. She was close to me now, but her gaze looked past me. Suddenly there was a terrific shriek close in my very ears, and I was awake. Startled and confused, I looked round and my eyes instinctively sought her berth. It was empty. The cabin was empty: the lamplight fell on the brass bolt of the door, still shot securely. A perfect, deep, unbroken silence lay heavily on all around me, and I was alone. One fearful, agonised glance round and I knew the truth. Like a madman, I sprang to the cabin door and tore it open. Thence I fled down the passage, up the companion stairs and reached the deck. The night was silent, moonless, and serene: in majestic state we were steaming

A Man's Life

eastwards between tranquil sea and sky. At
the head of the companion stair I gave a tremendous shout of "Man overboard," which
went echoing through the length and breadth
of the vessel. On the bridge a solitary figure
was pacing. It stopped suddenly. I looked
up. It was the captain.

"Harrison is overboard. Stop the ship," I
shouted to him madly as I rushed to the star-
board side and leaped over the light iron
railing.

After the first plunge, when I came to the
surface, I struck out as nearly as I could tell in
a direct line back over our course, straining my
eyes over the level expanse. Nothing met them
on every side but that horrible, black, serene,
and shimmering plain, swaying and undulating
in ripple behind ripple, smoothly and silently
rising and falling under the light of the stars.
A glance back at the red lights behind told
me I was already far astern of the ship. There
was a wild instinctive expectation in my brain
that I should find her. Each minute my straining eyes seemed to see a white arm raised for

help, my ears seemed breaking in an agonised listening for a cry, but I swam on, and there was nothing but the murmur of the water breaking at my neck; nothing before my eyes but the swelling upheaval of these perpetually rising and sinking smooth-breasted ripples. I shouted her name, and the boundless space seemed to mock me. There was no response but the soft lap of the water. Then it burst upon me in one sudden, blinding crash that I had lost her, irrevocably, utterly, finally. The conviction, the realisation came like the stroke of lightning, that I should never, could never find her. She had vanished beneath this level, limitless, trackless, superficies; it had closed over her, and she was gone from me for ever. Vanished—swallowed up in that smooth, black plain that would hold its secret eternally. She was beneath it somewhere, but where? where? I had no trace and no clue. Possessed by that delirious longing to escape from me, to hide herself from me, she had flung herself upon this wide, all-receiving bosom, and it had accepted her; she was folded to it in an ever-

A Man's Life

lasting oblivion. It would never give her up
to me. She was gone forth from me. She
had passed away out of my life, and left me
an undying reproach. And all our passion was
over, gone like the breath on a mirror. Never
throughout infinite time should I see that face,
or touch those lips, or hold that form again.
These things were now and for ever hence-
forward, of the past. I had lost her, and
through whose fault? What shall be said of
the man found asleep at his post? The stars
seemed rushing together over my head, the
heavens to descend and mingle with the waters.
I ceased to swim.

If I might sink to her side—if but this
heaving water would throw us together, though
it were but our two corpses that would meet in
a will-less embrace.

.   .   .   .   .   .

Sense came back to me when I was being
dragged on board ship. The boats, unable to
find her, had brought me back alone to the
horror of existence. I stood upright on the
deck, and knew that she was dead and I was

living. There was a good deal of confusion round me.

I saw a group of frightened-looking women huddled against the saloon door, and they stared at me. The men came round me. The captain and the doctor spoke to me. Then some one said, "What is it all?" And another said, "Was it an accident?" And another, "Look at his hand; look at the blood!" And another, "It seems as if there had been a struggle." And another, "Did he throw him out?" And another, "Perhaps he murdered him!" And I looked at them all and laughed, and the women shrank farther from me.

Murdered her! I thought. Not I, but the egoism of men's love, that gave birth to that delirious fear of me, instead of the sweet confidence and trust with which she should have come back to my arms. In her reasoning moments, indeed, I had been able to convince her, that of me, she need have no terror. Her death had been involuntary, I knew. Had not her last conscious words been, " I love you "?

A Man's Life

But in the delirium, the instinctive knowledge
of what men are, the intuitive sense of how
little strain their love will bear, and the dread
born of both, these had oppressed and haunted
her. Had I not watched these torturing her for
hour after hour as she raved to me about
myself? Still in my ears sounded those last
terrible soliloquies, those low-toned, delirious
confidences :—

"Cecil is not here—no—but when I go back
to him—it's no use going back if I've lost my
looks—I wish I had a glass here—where is
Hester ?—Hester, I would go to her—Hester
would always be nice to me—but men only care
for a woman for what they can get out of her—
their love is of no worth—you can't rely on
them—I can't meet him—no ; take me away
from him—I must get away—I know what his
voice will be—so cruelly cold—he thinks I
ought to have liked being shot, and as I didn't
he will not forgive me—he never has been cold
—no ; but then I was beautiful—Hester, I was
always considered beautiful, wasn't I ?—and I
knew how to play upon his feelings— he loved

his own pleasure—they are all alike—I doubt if
he could love impersonally—I wish I had a
glass—my face will disgust him—and the whole
thing—and then he'll talk about his honour—
men always do when they want to get rid of
a woman—and I can't live without him—
oh, Hester, Hester." And these thoughts had
murdered her.

I looked at the captain. "Kindly explain
this business, Mr. Ray," he said. I laughed
aloud.

"Explain?" I said. "What is there to explain? I was unable to keep awake any longer,
and while I was asleep he threw himself from
the window, as he had twice tried to do before
when delirious. For the rest, you can ask the
doctor if I were likely to murder him!" and I
turned away from them.

"For God's sake, watch him," I heard the
captain say, "or we shall have a suicide as well
as an accident."

Some young fellow followed me and took my
arm. I let him, and I walked on blindly up
the deck. He spoke to me. "Change your

clothes. . . . Let some one bind up your
wrist. . . ."

I neither understood nor answered.

We were going onward—onward and leaving her behind, and my life with her. And
the reproach within me seemed to wring my
soul. I neither regretted nor condemned my
passion for her: passion is the loved one's due
and the source of the loved one's pleasure. I
would not wish any love to be passionless; this
is for the moralists to urge. Passion and desire
are the very soul and vitality of love. It is
monstrous to strike at them; impossible to kill
them. But its egoism. This is an amorphous,
cancerous growth, and this consumes and eats
away the whole constitution of our love. Let
us cut this out. This had killed Theodora, as
it has killed, directly and indirectly, its millions.

When the dawn broke we came into Aden,
and they put me ashore—alone.

THE END.

THE WALTER SCOTT PUBLISHING CO., LIMITED, FELLING-ON-TYNE.

7·08